Reflection of the Forest

Avery W. Krouse

PublishAmerica

Baltimore

First printing

ISBN: 1-4137-1559-1
PUBLISHED BY PUBLISHAMERICA, LLLP
www.publishamerica.com
Baltimore

Printed in the United States of America

Dedicated to the memory of Gilbert and Betty Krouse, loving and providing in life and in spirit. To God, blessing me with each new surprise. To my cousin Brittany, my muse. And to the three friends, you know who you are and you know that I love you.

Table of Contents

Prologue

"I'm home!" Chris walked through the door, turning and locking it behind him. He flipped off the porch light, as he did every night after work. He wasn't very happy as a cashier at the local supermarket, but it was just a way to earn a little extra spending cash. Hearing no reply, he walked into the kitchen, pulling a can of cola from the refrigerator and heading towards his room at the back of the house. As he walked down the hall, he glanced at the pictures along the wall, seeing the one he almost hated passing each night. It was a specially made picture of his mother and father, one picture of each, side by side on one page. They had each been gone for a long time. His mother had passed away when he was eleven. She developed pneumonia after a long bout with cancer and, unfortunately, she didn't survive. He looked to the picture of his father. Everyone said he looked a lot like his father. His father had died just four months before Chris's sixteenth birthday, also after a bout with cancer. Their memories were fading from his, now, eighteen-year-old mind.

He stopped at his grandmother's door, hearing the soft snore coming from within. He moved in with her after his father's passing. Arching a brow, he looked at his watch. The reading of 11:00 told him it was later than he'd suspected. *I knew I shouldn't have stopped at that burger joint on the way home. I really need to keep better track of time*, Chris thought, pushing open his door and stepping in.

He opened the can of soda and took a drink as he walked over to his bunk bed. It was amazing; he had slept in this bed for nearly ten years. He was going to get rid of it for the sake of a more mature sleeping arrangement but the bed held so many memories for him that he just couldn't bear to do it. Every sleepover and play date from his childhood logged more hours using those bunks as the soldier's fort or the wizard's castle. He sat down on the bottom bed and started to think. It had been such a long day. "If they would only learn that it's such a hassle to use paper instead of plastic," he sighed to himself. He didn't even get any tips today.

As he flipped off his bedside lamp, he started to get a sinking feeling in the pit of his stomach. He knew he would have the dream again, the same dream he had had every night for the past few weeks. The dream tortured his evenings not because it was like some scene of a horror movie or held some powerful memories but it was just that he never finished it. He dreaded the night, knowing that he would never reach the end of the dream. It was there, all right, just beyond the blank pages, but the alarm roused him every morning before he could see the last part. He woke up in a cold sweat, his breath coming short. It was irrational, yes, but indescribable dread filled him as he lay down. Something inside him just couldn't understand why he would be so afraid. The dreams were so real, so realistic that he literally felt his fear and dread in his dream just as if he was awake. He sighed and closed his eyes, allowing his thoughts to settle and, in no time, was asleep.

"*Chris...*"

He looked up to see who called his name. No one was there. *How strange*, he thought. He continued to write.

"*Chris...*"

He looked up again, setting down his math book. Standing up, he peered outside his window, seeing if that was from where the voice had beckoned. No one was out there in the sunny backyard and Chris began to get suspicious. He walked over to his door and looked out into the hall. Still, no one was there.

"*Chris... come...*" He heard the strange voice again, as if it were just a whisper on the wind. All of a sudden it came to him. He slowly turned around to face his bed. Walking hesitantly toward it, he started to kneel to the floor beside it.

"It can't be," he thought out loud. He closed his eyes and slowly

8

reached underneath the bed, pulling out a tall, thin book that had been hidden in between the slats of the frame and the mattress. He sat the book down on his bed and stood up, staring at it.

"*Chris...come...*" The voice had grown stronger. A deep dark pressing feeling began to build within his stomach. The voice echoed in the pit of his heart filling him with an unsinkable anxiety.

He sat down beside the book, lifted it into his lap and slowly opened up the cover. Blank. He sighed a small sigh of relief and started to flip through the pages. They were all blank, just as they always had been. However, did he just imagine the voice? Shaking his head, he continued to flip through the pages, slowly edging closer to the back of the book. When he came near the back, he stopped, almost as it if weren't his will to do so. He slowly turned the page. It was blank. He turned another. Blank.

Again, he turned another, finding it blank as well. He came to the final page to turn. His forefinger and thumb grasped the edge of the very last page as a sweat broke across his brow. He slowly lifted it off the back cover of the book, turning his head and closing his eyes. In a quick motion he pushed the page to the other side, but did not turn back.

"*Now the time has come...*"

Chris gasped in fear as he slowly turned his head back. The final page was not blank at all. Upon it was a drawing, almost a simple sketch, which looked ancient in quality. He examined it closely, seeing that it was of four faces. Two men and two women now appeared on the page. The breeze from his window began to pick up as his head grew dizzy.

Suddenly, the breeze began to grow to a massive torrent of air that burst through his window. The sound of the current was so powerful that he had to cover his ears. That quick movement caused him to lose his support and the wind knocked him off the bed as the book flew out of his hands. He landed hard on his shoulder and downward against his stomach, knocking the breath out of him. At the moment of impact, his eyes shot open.

* * *

He was lying on his stomach on the floor beside his bed. He reached up, hitting the switch on his lamp. His pillows and bedcovers were strewn about the floor, and a light breeze was blowing through the window he couldn't remember having opened. He slowly rose up to his knees, rubbing his arm as he turned to pick up his sheet and blanket. He turned, placing the heap on his bed and turned back to the ground, suddenly freezing in place. He shook his head, denying the sight he just couldn't acknowledge. There, on the ground before him, was the book from his dream. He rubbed his eyes, thinking, *I must still be dreaming, oh God let me be dreaming.*

Chris reached out, touching its cover. It was real. He picked the book up and climbed to his feet. He took a seat on the bed and held the book solemnly in his hands. Could it be that he actually was holding the book from his unchanging dream? He couldn't actually remember ever looking under the slats of his bunk bed. In the ten years he owned that bed, he never once actually went under there. It suddenly occurred to him, though, that the accursed dream did change. He did get to that last, unreachable page. He did not want to open that book, but he knew he had to. Every fiber of his body fought against his fingers as they reached for the edge of the cover.

Slowly he lifted it open. There, the page that had once been blank, now was covered in ink. There were so many words written in a language that, although he had never seen it before, he strangely understood. He flipped through the book, each page covered with pictures, writings, and many different strange yet interesting things that he'd never seen before. He flipped back to the beginning of the book and focused his mind on the words at the top of the page. They seemed to become clear in his mind as he read them.

A voice too loud and too strong screamed through his mind. *"Now is the time. Gather the chosen. Come and set us free."* From the center of the page, a small circle began to glow. A small, glowing gray orb fell from it into Chris's hand.

As the orb touched his skin, everything rushed back to him. Memories, knowledge, pictures from his past, thousands and thousands of sounds and images tore through his brain causing him to clutch his head as the visions passed by his eyes. Apparitions of people he had never known, fields he had never crossed, mountains he had never climbed, they all filled his soul. He remembered what happened all those years ago. It had been blocked from his mind for so many years now, but he knew it all. One last image passed by his mind, a dark pair of eyes held by a completely shadowed face. The image shook him to the very center of his being. He knew, now, that the time had come.

1

The Chosen Four

Hearing the wake-up call from outside his door, Chris stood up. He wouldn't have been able to sleep anyway if he had tried, so he didn't. He walked out of his room and headed straight for the shower. Looking at himself in the mirror, he shook his head at his appearance. He had sabotaged his looks through many years of heavy eating, compounded by his lack of taste for healthy foods. His stomach jutted out well past him, hanging down from his chest and over his waist. It wasn't that he was that fat; it was just that he had quite the spare tire. Some described him as having a teddy-bear shape which he greatly preferred to some of the other words people had used to describe him in his time. He didn't fancy the rest of himself, either. His height was no more than some of the freshmen at his school, even though he himself was a senior. His face was rather large and round as well, offset by large glasses and the occasional pimple here or there. His hair was very short. He preferred it that way because he could never do anything with his hair when it was longer. He had been told that his glasses hid very nice blue-gray eyes and that his hair looked good when he spiked the bangs, but compliments were few and far between.

He looked over himself again in the mirror, sighing. His mind told him full and well that he was nothing to want to see. The depressing thoughts filled his mind every single time he looked into that condemning glass. There were very few times he could remember when he looked into one and actually approved of what he saw. Not many people knew the way he really felt about his appearance. Forever, he had longed to make some change, any change. "Today..."

He turned on the water, letting it heat up, and stepped in. A good scrub and shampoo later, he hopped out, brushed his teeth, put gel in his short brown hair, and did all the rest of his morning routine. Somehow it seemed fairly pointless, granted what he had on his plate for this afternoon. Stepping into the hall, the smell of his grandmother's home-cooked breakfast hit his nose. Heading to his room, he put on some random clothes and walked over to his bookshelf. He took from behind one of the volumes on his shelf a small plastic bag with several little things inside. He waved his hands over the top of it and said a few small words, the items inside glowing briefly before returning to normal. He walked over to the bed and picked up the old tome. He took the bag and the book and placed them inside his backpack, placing the pack around his shoulders and headed for the door.

He walked into the kitchen and sat down at the table, his grandmother already having a plate of his favorite, bacon, eggs, and toast, waiting for him. His grandmother was a rather short, elderly woman but she got around better than some people ten or twenty years younger than her. After he finished the meal, he kissed her goodbye and headed out the back door, walking out to his car.

"I don't want to do this to them. It's so unfair," he said to himself. Suddenly his mind flashed the image of the eyes. His body shook with the painful dread of that glare. He looked up to the clouds, begging to rid them of his mind as they slowly faded. Feeling a warm May morning wind, he hopped into his car and sped off. The drive to school was the longest he had ever experienced. The visions that had flown through his brain last night were still torturing him this morning. He knew that he had to bring upon his friends the same terror that he had to face. The thoughts of what was to come were so distracting that he actually ran a stop sign, though thankfully no other cars were in the area. In his little town, not many people were up and about early in the morning as most of the people went out of town to their jobs.

He pulled into his parking spot, parking a bit lopsidedly as he never could quite get the hang of it, and headed into the high school with a somber look on his face. He looked at his watch, his walk now taking on a bit more speed. The day had started and, as far as what had to be done was concerned, he was fairly on top of things. He walked into the commons area, seeing the usual morning run of people and smiling and waving at a few as he went along. He walked into the cafeteria, grabbed an orange juice, paid for it, and went to sit at his usual table. "Good morning," he said through a smile at his friends. Chris turned to Darla Phillips with a forced smile. "And a glorious good morning to you!"

Darla smiled back, pushing some of her shoulder-length, blonde hair behind her ear, and replied, "Good morning to you too. Big Chemistry test today. You ready?"

With a nod, he leaned back in his chair. "I'm not really worried about it."

She gave him a strange look, her brown eyes sparkling, then giggled lightly and smiled. "Oh you. Just because you are good at Chemistry..."

"Me? Good at Chemistry? That's funny," he interrupted. "I simply get the formulas and functions, that's all." He chuckled and took a sip of his juice. He looked to his watch, his eyes lit up, and he smiled. "I just remembered. I have something for you!"

"Oh?" she asked, a smile lighting her face in minor anticipation.

He nodded and reached inside his backpack into a small plastic bag. Pushing aside the gray orb within, he took out a small golden bracelet. The chain was adorned in the middle with a small blue gem set in a rose-shaped plate. "Here. I saw this in a little shop up on the strip and thought of you."

She smiled, blushing just a bit, and extended her hand to him. He smiled and clasped the bracelet around her wrist. She jerked her hand back as a small spark popped out from the bracelet. "Oh! Darned static electricity." She examined it, smiling at the simple beauty.

* * *

Before Chris started to speak, his friend Donnie Johnson, a fairly tall, muscular young man, sat down beside him. He dropped the plate of biscuits and gravy on the table and took off his jacket, slinging it into the chair beside him. "Of course, you get her a present and not me. I see how you are," he said in a mocking voice.

"I don't sound like that," retorted Chris. "And besides, I did get you something too." He reached down into the bag and pulled out a small patch.

"What did ya get me?"

Chris handed him the small patch bearing the emblem of his choir department. He looked at his watch then smiled back to Donnie. "The directors are giving these to all the students who passed the audition for the state summer clinic to wear during the trip."

Donnie's jaw dropped as a great big smile crosses his face. "You're joking, right? Cool!"

"Yep. If you had been here yesterday instead of faking sick to avoid our English test," he said with a grin and scoffed, "you would have gotten them. Catie and Darla made it also. Of course, the best singer in the department also made it."

"Let me guess," he replied, rolling his eyes.

"Indeed, 'twas the one and only: me."

Donnie chuckled and placed the patch in his jacket pocket. He then picked up his fork but quickly dropped it, a spark catching his fingers as well.

"Hey, you know, that happened to me too," Darla remarked.

Donnie shook his head and shrugged, scratching his red head. Picking up his fork again, he smiled as nothing happened then started to eat. "Besides, I didn't fake sick yesterday. I just didn't have the project done that went along with the test. I seem to remember someone else doing the very same thing last month over the poetry unit."

"I did not," Chris replied. "It was just a whole lot of poetry to analyze. Frankly, I would have gotten a better grade if my stupid computer hadn't crashed in the middle of the night."

"Well, if you didn't wait until the middle of the night before a project is due to actually start working on it, you would actually score higher than you do. I doubt I would have even gotten mine done without Catie's help."

"Ah yes, but who made the A plus on his hero report, the A plus on his computer presentations for *Scarlet Letter*, an A—"

"Thank you, Chris, that will be quite enough," replied Donnie, stuffing his face with a gravy-covered chunk of biscuit.

"Speaking of Caitlyn, have any of you seen her around?" asked Chris as he glanced to his watch.

"Yeah. She was headed toward the math hall, I think," Donnie answered. Chris smiled and nodded, standing up, grabbing his backpack, and heading off without a word.

"Hmm. What's with him?"

Donnie shook his head to Darla's question. "I don't know. Hasn't he been acting weird lately?"

"Yeah, I think so. He seems to be very nervous first thing in the morning. I remember he said something about not getting much sleep. Maybe he's just getting anxious about college junk." Darla nodded and looked to her bracelet, smiling softly to herself.

Chris walked through the commons and to the front lobby, looking around a bit for Caitlyn, but not seeing her, decided it would be best to just wait and catch her later. "Plenty of time. No need to rush," he tried to assure himself. Just then, he turned to see Caitlyn Bible walking towards him from the way he came.

"Hey, I walked into the cafeteria and Donnie said you were looking for me. Said you went down this way. What is it?"

Chris smiled softly at her. "Oh, nothing really. I wanted to return your clipboard. I forgot to meet you after school so, you know, I just figured you might need it." She nodded to him as he took off his backpack and reached for her clipboard.

"You know, I waited around for you for a half-hour yesterday afternoon," she said.

"I'm very sorry. They called my cell phone and wanted me in early to work. I tried to get Rachel to tell you. Did she not find you?"

"No, she never did. Eh, she does get a bit side-tracked at times." He handed the clipboard to her but as it touched her hand, she stepped back as a small spark flew out from the metal of the clip. "You know, that seems to be happening a lot today. Darla and Donnie both got shocked when I handed them something. Guess it must just be my electric personality, eh?" Caitlyn chuckled and took the clipboard, removing her backpack and stooping over to open it and put in the board.

As she stood back up, about the same height as him, she brushed a bit of her long, red hair behind her ear and smiled to him. "Shall we head to the cafeteria?" he asked.

"Yeah, sure."

They stepped into the cafeteria; the room was noisy as usual. Walking over to the table Chris had just recently left, Caitlyn said good morning to Donnie and Darla, the others that had been there already gone. Chris pulled out a chair for Caitlyn and smiled at her as she sat down. "Thank you, Chris," she said sweetly.

Donnie opened his mouth with a cocky grin on his face and prepared to tease Chris but he flung up his hand to preempt. "Ah! Don't want to hear it." Caitlyn chuckled and looked at Chris for a second before turning to Donnie to start up a conversation.

"Are you getting all of your college things finished, Chris?" asked Darla.

"Well, yes and no. It's kind of complicated. College may not be an option for me anymore."

"Why not? You had your heart set on it so much. It's all you've been talking about for months now."

"Like I said, it's very complicated. See, something happened last night. I finally got to sleep and—"

"Yes, you have been having trouble there, haven't you?" she interrupted.

"Yeah, I've been having this dream lately. You see—" He was interrupted again by the sounding of the morning bell.

* * *

18

As the bell finished its chime, the four began to disperse to go to their first period classes. Chris stopped them before they left, saying, "There's something I have to tell you, but I can't until I have enough time. Please come back to this table for lunch."

"What is it, Chris?" Darla asked.

"I can't really tell you right now, but it is very, very important." The other three nodded and went off to their classes. Chris lingered for a second, reaching into his backpack for the small gray orb. He saw no sign of activity within it and sighed a bit of hesitant relief. He placed it back into his backpack and headed to the front office.

He walked in the door of the front office, setting his books down against the wall to one side. "Good morning!"

"Good morning, Chris," replied Judith, the secretary.

"Got any jobs for me to do, Miss Judy?" he asked.

"Yes, start on the announcements now. I've got some errands for you to run," said the secretary with a smile as the phone rang. She picked it up and began to take a message.

"I'll get right on that." He walked behind the desk and sat in his chair at the office computer. He'd used it nearly every day to type the daily announcements and other things since he had become an office aide at the beginning of the semester. He pulled the file up and took the stack of announcements, beginning to put the new ones in and take the old ones out. It wasn't very tedious work. The school used a very simple computer system. They had actually changed it once but it gave the teachers and students so many problems that they returned to the old one in short order. He actually once ended up having the same teacher for five different classes during one year. It was rather amusing but they got everything cleared up. His high school life had been filled with many interesting events as it progressed. He held many fond memories, many fond and now fleeting memories. With a sigh, he continued his computer work.

* * *

Once he had finished with those, the secretary gave him a stack of papers that had to be delivered to every teacher. He took them and walked out the door, heading down one hall. Room after room, he took a paper to each. It was very monotonous work, but he was generally well liked by the faculty at his school, mostly due to his hard-earned reputation as a good guy. Everybody understood that he was the go-to guy to get something done and always held a smile and good word for each member of the faculty. It wasn't that he was a brownnoser or anything like that; he just generally liked the people he studied under. Each teacher greeted him as he entered and exited each room. As he walked down the hall, he reached into his pocket, taking out the orb again. It was still lifeless. He placed it back in his pocket.

He walked into the one of the history classrooms, handing the paper to the teacher with a smile. She placed it in a folder on her desk. As he was walking out, he noticed Darla sitting in the back of the class. He nonchalantly pretended to fiddle through the papers while taking his glance at her. She was writing something that looked like a note, but he noticed that her writing seemed very slow as occasionally she would stop and seem to stare at the bracelet on her wrist. Knowing what was to come, he couldn't help but feel a small bit of regret that the peace she now felt probably wouldn't remain. She looked up for a brief second or two, glancing at Chris with a smile and small wave. He smiled back and walked out.

As the bell rang, Chris picked up his backpack and got ready to head to his next class. He said goodbye to the secretary, giving her a light hug, even though she couldn't quite understand why, and walked out. Heading upstairs, he walked into his English class and sat down at the desk. Darla sat in the desk next to him and Donnie sat behind her. He reached into his pocket once more, bringing the orb under his desk as he glanced at it. It seemed to be an ordinary glass ball. He was about to put it away when he noticed a pulse of light, very short, and very dull, escaping the orb. *Oh no*, he thought, his mind racing. *It's happening. It can't be happening yet! We're not all*

together! His breath became short as he began a nervous sweat.
"What's wrong, Chris? You seem worried about something?"
asked Darla.

"It's nothing. I'm just—um, yeah, I forgot to read the assignment
from yesterday. That's what it is. It's the second time this week I've
forgotten to read one of them and I'm getting a little behind."

"Well hey, if you need to go over some of it, we can meet after
school and read through it, if that would help?"

"No, no," he replied, staring at the orb he held below the desk.
"I'll make it up."

He placed the orb back in his pocket, wiping a bit of sweat from
his brow. He sat through the class, anxiously awaiting the end of the
period. He was not able to pay any attention to his book, the teacher,
or anything else going on in the room. A couple of times during the
lesson, Donnie had to tap him on the shoulder to knock him out of the
times he zoned out. It wasn't very long before Chris asked to use the
restroom and was excused.

As he stepped outside the door, he leaned against the wall,
catching his breath. "You're going to have to calm down, Chris, or
you'll never make it. Class ends in just twenty minutes," he said to
himself. He stepped over to take a drink from the water fountain and
collect himself. He walked back into class and sat down in his desk.

It seemed to take an exceptionally long time but eventually the
bell rang. As he was lost in his thoughts, it made him jump, his mind
beginning to race again, and he quickly left the room, heading toward
the cafeteria.

"What is with him? I swear! That boy is jumpy today," said
Donnie, grabbing his backpack.

"Let's go talk to him. Maybe he's coming down with something,"
said Darla. The two walked out and down toward the cafeteria.

Chris entered the noisy hall and sat down at the usual table, not
even bothering to get anything to eat. One by one, the three
eventually joined him. Reaching into his pack, he pulled out the
small gray orb and concealed it between clasped hands. "I think there

is something I should tell you guys." He looked at the orb out of their view, seeing it start to glow faintly as a nervous sweat broke across his brow.

"Chris? What is it? You haven't been yourself today," Darla said, placing a hand on his shoulder.

"See, I've been having this dream—" He paused, looking down at the orb. "I was told something that—" He paused again as he began to feel the orb pulsate within his hands. He breathed a deep sigh. "Oh God, there isn't enough time to explain." They looked to each other with puzzled looks came over their faces. Chris looked at the orb one last time, seeing it start to shimmer brightly before he took a deep breath. "I'm so sorry, you guys. Please, please forgive me! I'm sorry I couldn't prepare you…"

A glare now fell over his eyes as he looked to the rafters of the cafeteria, starting to mumble small, indistinct words. "Chris? What are…?" The words fell from Caitlyn's mouth as a small hush fell over the rest of the cafeteria. The calm before the storm was soon broken, as Chris's chanting became louder, the words, though clearer, still unintelligible.

"Chris, what is wrong with you?" asked Donnie as Chris's head started to level. The air seemed charged around him, the words still pouring from his mouth, becoming louder and louder. The three began to back in their chairs, pushing away from the table.

Chris shot up to his feet, seeming taller now, and raised his hands, placing the orb between the thumb and forefingers of each hand, the shimmer becoming brighter now. Every face turning to the now screaming young man, murmurs began spreading like wildfire. A couple of teachers had already started heading over to silence the young man.

Suddenly, he called out at the top of his lungs, "*Kredala nil sictu daram! Kredala nil sictu daram!*" He continued to call out the chant again and again as a strong wind blew in through the windows. The gray orb suddenly disappeared with a blinding flash.

The lips of a boy at the table beside them abruptly became still as his voice faded. Another voice ceased, and another, and yet another as silence and stillness was spreading throughout every person in the room, save Chris's table, who now looked at him with fear in their eyes. He was still standing, his hair, now bluish-white, hung down to his shoulder blades, blowing in the dark breeze.

The noise started to drop around the room, person after person starting to become rigid. Caitlyn, Donnie, and Darla looked around the room, starting to become frantic at what was going on. Soon, everybody in the room was frozen at their tables, some standing around, staring blankly toward where Chris had stood, mouths agape, fingers pointing. Some hands dropped forks and spoons; others dropped backpacks and books. After a while, all motion in the room had stopped. Only the three before Chris were left awake as his chant started to drop. Chris fell back into his chair, breathing hard, his body seeming to change with every breath.

Donnie had stood to his feet, Caitlyn and Darla soon following, and the three began rushing around the room, checking the bodies for anyone who might have remained sentient. Darla was the first to run out into the commons, seeing the still bodies scattered across the room, in the halls, everywhere the eyes could see. Caitlyn met her out there as did Donnie and the three stood gazing around the room in shock. They heard a door behind them opening and they turned to see a strange person approaching them.

2

Understanding

"I am sorry to have scared you so much, but it had to be done." The voice that spoke the words was deeper now, older, that of a new young man.

Donnie stepped between him and the girls. "You stay the hell away from us! What did you just do and who the hell are you?"

"Calm down, Donnie! It's me, Chris," the young man said, stepping toward them.

"You just back off, pal! I don't know what you did or what that was but you are not Chris," yelled Darla. "Stay away!"

"Donnie, Darla, Caitlyn, it's me. I am Chris, the same guy you've always known. Please calm down and let me explain."

The three of them turned to run away but Chris raised his hands causing them to stop in place. He walked around to the front of them as they were locked in their running pose though still able to see, hear, etc. "Now look, I am your friend Chris, the guy you've known since high school. I played on the playground with you in elementary school, I was in the play last semester; I'm the same guy. Donnie, you used to put me in wrestling locks and I'd scream like a little girl. Do you guys know me now? Blink at me if you do."

The three of them blinked at him and he waved his hand, causing them to resume motion. They stopped themselves and stood, staring blankly at the tall, lean figure.

He motioned to a nearby room and said, "Let's just go in here and

I'll explain things."

Donnie paced around the teachers' lounge, sipping water from a paper cup. "Okay, I'll accept that you're my best friend. But I have to know something. What was that?"

Chris looked toward Caitlyn and Darla, who sat on the lounge couch beside a frozen teacher, still shaking a bit. "Magic."

Darla turned to him, still amazed and yet frightened at what happened. "Magic? You mean, like witchcraft?"

Chris shook his head to her. "No, most witchcraft is small time stuff. I am assuming that the power I've got is that of a higher persuasion."

Caitlyn stared at him a bit before speaking. "Well, whatever that was, everyone in the building is frozen, except for us. Did you do that too?"

Chris nodded. Darla couldn't take her eyes off him. Everything about him had changed. He now stood much taller, thinner, with a slimmer profile. His eyes were a piercing deep blue and his hair, now to the base of his shoulder blades was a bright white, streaked with sapphire. He was now dressed in a bright green tunic, almost a tee shirt but buttoned up the front, and dark blue twill pants. Now hung on his back from around his neck was a dark blue robe, hooded and tied at the neck and waist. The almost medieval appearance reminded her of someone she would have seen in a movie or play. He had changed so much from how he used to look. It was almost as if he was a different person.

"I cast a spell on you. I had a few instructions. Remember earlier, when I made contact with each of you through means of an item? The clipboard, the patch, the bracelet? The spark was not really static electricity. I was supposed to say a few words over things that you were to touch and that would somehow act as a sealer. I guess that whatever it was had to be metal." He looked to Donnie for a second. "That's why yours didn't take effect until you touched the fork, but it was the patch for you. I needed you three to remain awake."

"Why us?" asked Darla. The words echoed in the minds of all three for a moment until a deep sigh from Chris's lips broke the silence.

"I saved you because we have been called to rescue the world."

Donnie turned to Chris and stammered, "Called to rescue…the world? What is that supposed to mean?"

"You'd better sit down with the girls."

Chris looked to them silently for a bit, and then spoke. "Apparently, it was revealed to me several years ago that there is some kind of problem in an alternate, but similar world. This problem was described as 'the darkness' and drains the life out of people. It's more that they are taken over by it. No one seems to be immune except us."

Darla sat, taking this in. *Is this really true? Is this a dream?* she thought. She turned to Chris and asked, "Okay, well, why are we the ones you chose to keep awake?"

"It really was more of a calling. I have had this dream for so long and, when it finally came to me, it was like this surge of memory just exploded within me. When everything unlocked in my mind, I knew that it was the three of you."

"Okay, then why are you the only one who has changed at all?" asked Donnie.

He walked over to the couch and sat on the arm beside Darla. "My talent came to me when needed. I am apparently a wizard, a wielder of arcane power. Each of you, too, shall have your own design for this new time in our lives. It will come to you upon the first use. Unfortunately, a lot of things come with it."

Donnie turned to him, saying, "Do you know? Do you know what each of us will become?"

Chris shook his head. "I think you must not know who you truly are until you become them or you will reject your gift. This is the way it must be."

The four of them walked through the back hall doors and out into the courtyard. "…So I walked into the shop and there he was, this really old man, stooped over at the desk. I looked around a bit, you know, browsing while my mom hung out with her friends in the restaurant. Even back then, my folks trusted me a lot. I was free to roam the shops as long as I didn't go off the block. This store seemed interesting, it had like beads and candles and figurines in the window so I went in.

"It was about sunset when I saw this dark, silver ball, about the size of a soccer ball, sitting on a strange looking stand." They crossed over to the gym and went inside, stepping over a few sleeping bodies as they went. They sat on the bleachers and continued to listen to Chris. "I couldn't resist the ball. It looked so cool. I placed my hands on it and there was this, like, electricity flowing through it, like one of those static balls. It was weird. The electricity just surged through my body. The man at the desk walked over to me and pulled my hands off the ball, holding them in his own. He smiled and nodded to me and said, 'You're the one,' and led me to this room in the back of the store. I had some strange compulsion to just follow." Donnie had stood up and descended down to the floor, walking around a bit, still attentive, though.

"He told me the darkness story and then waved his hands over my eyes. I think my mind must have locked everything out because I couldn't remember any of this until last night. I've been having this strange dream every night about this book." Chris waved his hand in the air in a pulling motion, a thin book appearing in his hand as if he had pulled it off a shelf. "All of a sudden, I woke up and there the book was. Check this out." He flipped to the back of the book and showed the girls the last page with the drawing of the faces of each one of the four.

Each picture seemed very similar to what they looked like now, but more advanced. Chris was in his advanced state now, as his picture showed well. Donnie joined them again and looked on with them. "See, that's us, the four of us here. This page seemed to stand out to me and I just…knew that it was the four of us. That's why I had to get us all together and cast my spell. Time had to cease so that we would be able to work unnoticed and so that the rest of the world would not continue on making things worse."

27

"The rest of the world?" Darla asked. "You mean the entire world is frozen?"

Chris nodded. "Everyone is basically asleep and still. It was practically the only way this could come about. I read this last night." He flipped a few pages and began to read. "The four shall be born unto this world as children, but shall leave this world as men, born and reborn with the calling of the ancients."

"We don't belong here, guys. You've felt it too, haven't you? A calling. A deeper longing to be somewhere else." They slowly nodded in agreement. "I've done further reading and, although the book does not elaborate very much, I have discovered something. We're not of this world. Yes, we were born here, but we don't belong here. There's another world. It's the world from which this darkness is coming, the place where the darkness began." The three of them continued to listen, entranced by his words, so familiar, they knew it was true.

"Unfortunately, it's not satisfied. Whoever or whatever is controlling the darkness knows about us, knows about this world. It's been feeding off the evil and hatred in this world, but it isn't enough. The darkness has discovered a way in and it's coming. We only have a short time before it comes here. We must find a way into our true world and stop the darkness. It will kill those here much quicker because this world is already weakened by its own vice."

Caitlyn turned to Chris, arching a brow. "But if we go there, won't we get weakened by the darkness? I mean, we've grown up here, but aren't we weak too?"

Chris shook his head, saying, "The book says that we're the only people that *can* withstand the darkness for a long time. It has something to do with the spirit that fills me now and the ones that you will receive. However, if we don't succeed, both worlds will be doomed."

"As I had said, we have to find a way to get back to our world. I've read this whole book cover to cover and I still can't find a way. It's ridiculous. This book is telling us that we have to get to our real home and the stupid thing doesn't even say how we are supposed to do so!" Chris sighed and paced across the gym floor. "I think that it would take a great amount of magic to open a portal between our two worlds. Unfortunately, I don't know the spell, it's not in the book, and I don't believe I'd have the power anyways. I don't know how I pulled off the sleeping spell, but I think it was because of that casting orb." They joined Chris on the floor and started to walk out into the sunlight of the courtyard.

Donnie thought for a while before saying, "Well, maybe one of us has magical powers too. Do we?"

Chris shrugged, saying, "I really don't know. It's very possible. The book is kind of limited on the information it gives. In fact, I noticed that many of the pages in the book were either faded, torn out, or otherwise unreadable." They nodded and continued to talk.

"What about our families?" Caitlyn asked. "What has happened to them?"

Chris patted her back to reassure her. "Don't worry, they are just fine. Suspended like everyone else."

"Can we go back and check on them?"

"Yes, of course. According to a spell I found in the book, I can teleport you all to your homes. Finish up your business and get everything in order. Call out my name when you wish to return. I will remain here. I already know how my family is doing."

Caitlyn walked to Chris's side, taking his hand. "Then will you come with me? I don't really want to be by myself."

Chris smiled, patting her hand, and nodded. "Of course I will. On that thought, Donnie, why don't you accompany Darla as well? I'll send you two to Donnie's first, then, when you call out to me, I'll hear you, I think, and I'll send you to Darla's. All right?" Donnie and Darla nodded and stood beside each other. Chris raised his hand to the sky and started to chant. A deep blue glow encased Darla and Donnie as they began to fade out. Darla clasped Donnie's hand just as they faded from sight.

"Our turn?" Chris smiled to Caitlyn and nodded. Chanting softly, he took her hand and they faded out as well.

Another faint blue shimmer and Caitlyn and Chris appeared in her house. "Boy, if only I could have traveled this way long before now. Would have saved a lot of time and gas, that's for sure." She chuckled and stepped out into the house, starting to walk around a bit. He walked to her kitchen and sat down at the table, waving up a glass of tea, sipping lightly.

Caitlyn walked down the hall to her parents' bedroom. Her mother was lying there on the bed frozen in her sleep, as if she had never gotten up at all. "You didn't go to work today, did you? You were planning on sleeping in. Looks like you got your wish." She walked to the bedside and sat down, taking her mother's hand. "You would be proud of me, Mom. I just know it. Your daughter is going to save the world. At least, I hope we will." She gently stroked her mother's hair. She paused, taking a deep breath. "God, Mom, I don't know what to think anymore. This has happened so fast. Just this morning I was sitting in my first period class, blissfully unaware that there was any damned darkness or anything else wrong with the world. I almost wish none of this had ever happened. It's so surreal! Maybe Chris's dream is still going on and I'm just a character in it.

"You remember Chris? He's got magical powers now. He's the one who made me aware of who I really am and what all has happened. You should see him; he has changed so much," she said, chuckling softly. She took the hand again and kissed it softly. "Well, he's waiting for me. I have to go now. I really hope to return soon." Tears began to form in her eyes. "I love you so much, Mom…" Caitlyn stood, pulled the blanket up over her mother and walked out, closing the door.

She walked back into the living room, looking for her dad. "Oh yeah, he'd be at work." Caitlyn sighed softly to herself and decided not to ask, wiping a tear from her eye. "I don't think I could take having to say goodbye again." Her thoughts were deep as she walked into the kitchen.

"Are you all right? I know this is tough, but we will make it through."

Caitlyn nodded to Chris as an answer and walked over, sitting beside him. "Will they be all right? What happens if we take too long?"

"Well, they are pretty much in a state of suspended animation. They won't age, they won't hunger, they won't thirst, etc. I don't think they have anything to worry about."

She nodded and took his hand again. "I'm scared Chris. What happens when we get over there, if we get over there? We could be killed, or we may fall to the darkness, or something else...there are just way too many questions."

"I know, Catie. I understand. I was up all night pacing around my room, pondering everything that might happen. I have thought and rethought over the idea of that darkness. I know how much danger we are blindly walking into and, yes; I have given consideration to our possible demise. I do, however, honestly believe that we'll succeed. I can't doubt it, otherwise it won't happen."

"Yeah, but that doesn't make me any less afraid."

A blue light appeared in the office where Donnie's father worked. Two people stepped from within it as it faded away. Donnie looked around, spotting his father, staring blankly at his desk. Donnie walked over to him, Darla staying where she appeared, watching silently. Donnie gently sat down beside his father and began to speak softly. "I know, I know. I could just hear you saying, 'Donnie, you can't go save the world with Chris until you clean your room.' Well, I haven't cleaned my room, but I don't think it's going to matter. This may be the last time I get to see you, Dad. I think you'd be so proud of me." Donnie paused for a moment, fighting back tears, hearing a faint sniffle from the girl behind him. "There were so many things I could have done before to show you how much I love you and Mom. I wish I...if only I had..." Donnie paused again, this time not being able to fight as hard, a few tears collecting at his eyes. Darla stepped up behind him and gently placed her hand on his shoulder. He grasped it lightly and continued, thankful for her support. "You'll be proud of me, though. I…we…my friends and I, we're going to go save the world. I could never live if something happened to you, Dad, or to Mom. I have to go see Mom now. Please sleep well. I will be back for you, someday." Donnie turned to Darla and smiled softly at her as she wiped a tear away from his cheek. He nodded to her and stood up, looking to the sky. "Chris, send me to my mother!" His voice echoed in the room as the faint blue shimmer covered them once more and in an instant, they were gone.

Chris dropped his hand from the air, closing the spell. "Donnie's gone to his mother's now. He's already seen his father. Just thought you might want to know."

Caitlyn nodded to him and sat there silently for a short while. Finally, she decided to speak. "You've had this secret inside you for a very long time now, haven't you? You just never knew."

"I guess so, yes. I don't really know why I was chosen, or for that matter, why any of the four of us was chosen. I figure it was just bound to happen to someone and it happened to us. It's just been inside of us all our lives. I don't think I could have taken knowing all this and never being able to do anything about it."

She looked at him for a minute, many more thoughts flowing through her head now. This boy, this young man, whom she had known since they were in kindergarten together, was given a destiny that no one on earth could have predicted. He used to be so timid, so meek. He was bullied by the other kids for being so different and yet all this time, he has had power beyond comprehension. She now looked into his eyes, the eyes that now gleamed with new strength, with new courage. It was almost as if she was looking into the eyes of a complete stranger, yet his presence was so familiar to her, so warm and comforting.

The young man that had once been her best friend was now truly a different person, on the outside. She knew, though, that the same love of life, the same spark, the same compassion, everything she admired and trusted in this person was still there. In some ways, everything had really changed. In others, he was still the same.

Chris raised his hand again, the light coating it again then fading. "They're on to Darla's house now." Caitlyn nodded to him. Then she smiled.

3

Cleric's Calling

Stepping from the light, Darla and Donnie found themselves in the den of Darla's home. They walked from the room and sought out her parents. They first found her mother, frozen on the couch. Darla sat down beside her and took her hand. "Well, Mom, I can't really believe what has happened. I've gone from worrying about my grades to worrying about my very next breath." Tears formed in her eyes now, tears of sadness, but also of regret and pain. "In one small leap, I've been shoved into a situation where I could end up forfeiting my very existence for the rest of the world. It seems so unfair! I don't want to die! I don't want to lose you, either! If we don't make it, my whole family, my friends, everyone I care about will be dead! I can't take knowing that it could depend on me, Mom! I can't…I…"

She broke down now, her tears flowing freely. Donnie stepped to her side and put an arm around her. She sobbed a bit, standing. "Shh…shh…it will be okay, Darla. Everything will be fine…" She sobbed once more, starting to quiet a bit. "You think I'd let anything happen to you? I've known you forever! I will be there to make sure we succeed. So will Chris and Caitlyn. Now, you buck up, okay?" She slowly stopped crying and looked up into his eyes, nodding softly. "Now, let's go find your father and let you say goodbye to him as well." Nodding again, she stood up, leaning over to kiss her mother's cheek before starting to walk again. She slowly made her way down a hall toward the back of the house, Donnie following behind her. Stopping at a door, she grabbed the handle, turned to look at Donnie for reassurance briefly, and turned the knob, pushing the door open. With a scream, she raced into the room.

Donnie, startled, rushed up to the doorway, seeing Darla kneel beside the figure of her father. He came in quickly, dropping to his knees beside the man. There was a small wound on his head just above the ear and a pool of dried blood beside his head. Donnie looked around the area, seeing a chest of drawers just to their side, a bit of red around one of the corners. "How could this have happened? Why wasn't he frozen in place?" Donnie shouted. "My God, he must have hit his head before the spell!"

Darla wasn't really paying attention to him, focused solely on her father. She pressed her ear to his chest, hearing a faint heartbeat. She tried to think back to her first aid class back in middle school, but that was so long ago, it was hard to remember any of it. She remembered how to start CPR, though, and quickly pressed her hands to his chest.

Donnie looked at her, saying, "Darla, he's frozen, he—"

She started to pump her hands in the bottom center of his rib cage. Tears started to flow from her eyes as she began to pray. Her cries to God slowly became audible, as she no longer cared who heard her. Strangely, though, her words became jumbled, almost pushed together. They began to change into a strain of words that were unknown to her before. Her hands began to take on an almost glowing quality as she spoke, the words becoming crisper, clearer, but still unfamiliar.

Donnie looked at Darla, his eyes starting to go wide as the sight before him. "Darla, what are you doing?" She looked at him quickly, shaking her head in frightened confusion. Her eyes were filled with a look letting Donnie know she was no longer in control. Looking back to her father, she saw a faint stir in his body, her hands glowing deeper now. The white light that surrounded her hands began to escape them in small tendrils that wrapped themselves around her arms. She continued to chant, closing her eyes as the glow started to enter her father's body. Donnie noticed that as Darla began to glow, she seemed to get a little taller. As she continued to chant, a rush of wind blew into the room, sweeping over her body as thousands of images and sounds began to flood her head, causing her to clutch her ears and scream. The sight of the terrifying eyes piercing into her mind caused her to faint.

As Darla fell to the ground beside her father, the pool of blood at his head began to disappear, as did the wound at his temple....

"Chris, haven't you noticed something?"

"You too? It's been nearly an hour since they last called!"

Caitlyn nodded to him and stood up. Chris followed suit. "Can you take us to them?" Chris had already begun to chant as he raised his hands. As he chanted, Caitlyn noticed that the blue glow, which was normally quick to appear, now became apparently slower to shine. She pondered this thought as the two of them began to disappear.

Stepping out of the portal into the living room, Caitlyn called out to Darla and Donnie, hearing a reply from the back of the hall. Chris stepped out behind her and closed down the gateway. As Caitlyn headed down the hall, Chris sat down on the couch and laid back, feeling rather tired.

Caitlyn walked down the hall to the open door of the bedroom. She walked in, noticing Donnie leaning against the wall and a man she assumed was Darla's father lying on the bed. "Why were you guys gone so long?"

Donnie stood up straight and said, "We found out who the other magic user is." He motioned to the door. From behind it, a young lady stepped out and greeted Caitlyn. She looked strangely familiar, though Caitlyn couldn't quite place her. She did, though, look a bit like....

A young woman now stood before Caitlyn, a bit taller than herself. Her hair was a bit wavy and was a bright blond shade. It came down to her cheeks just below her ears. Her eyes were brown, as they had always been, but they were a bit brighter now. In fact, she seemed to glow herself, as if the light came from within her fair skin.

She was cloaked in a bright, white robe that opened in the front as was tied in cross-strands across the neck and chest. Below that were a simple white blouse and a knee-length lavender skirt. Caitlyn gasped slightly as it hit her.

"She—Donnie, that's…"

The young woman nodded. Donnie chuckled and said, "Yes, this beautiful young lass is Darla. It scared me at first 'cause she collapsed."

"How…?"

"Sit down," Darla said, "and we'll tell you the whole thing."

"…And then we lifted him up into the bed and tucked him in." Caitlyn nodded to her and sighed a bit. "Hmm. Well, it isn't a big surprise. I knew it wouldn't be me. I'm not that special."

"Yes you are," came a voice from behind her. "You all are very special in your own ways. We are a team, each with their own talents that will end up being great assets to us. Of course, we just don't know the talents of the other two. However, we do now have a new Darla, I see." Chris stepped in, noticing the new Darla and smiling a bit.

"Where have you been?" asked Donnie.

"I had to rest on the couch for a bit. I'll explain later. For now, though," he said as he walked to Darla and took her hand, "we have much to discuss, my dear."

The four of them were sitting in the living room as Chris began to talk about the events that unfurled. "According to the book, my power is brought from within me through a catalyst. That small orb I held when I cast the time freeze spell was called a 'casting orb.' I have to have a specific one of those every time I want to cast a specific spell, unless I have the spell written in a spell book, in which case I can cast it straight from a chant or gesture. I'm not precisely sure how to inscribe spells into a book, though, or for that matter, how to get a hold of any orbs. I guess we must find them or buy them or something like that, but there are tons of spells in the book for the meantime. Anyways, that's how I cast spells. It's the same with you, Darla." He stood up and walked over to one wall. "Of course, the catalyst for magic is our own inner force. The heavier the spell, the higher the drain, so I couldn't just keep tossing out as many spells as I had orbs for."

They nodded a bit as Darla spoke. "So that's why you get tired out? All the casting you've done today would take it out of you, I'm sure."

He chuckled. "You don't know the half of it, but you will. Teleportation is a rather heavy spell and I've been flinging it around all day. Your power comes in a similar form. However, certain things affect our powers. For example, if we are together, we kind of draw from each other. If you are in a bright place, or near a church or anything of the holy nature, your power goes up. As for me, there are certain places for me that will increase my power, such as when any mages get together for ritual magic."

Darla nodded. "Well, if you are a wizard and you cast spells like you do, then what am I? What kinds of stuff do I do?"

"Well, I don't know the exact range of your spells. I do know that all your spells are of the defense and support nature. You are called a cleric, a priestess. Your power comes from a nature similar to mine but of a more holy genre. You do have several healing spells written down in your spell book but I think that the spell that transformed you is most likely way too powerful for you in your normal state. By that same token, I don't think I could cast another time freeze of that magnitude. That one's not even in the book."

Darla nodded again, twisting a bit of her hair around a finger. "This is all rather confusing. I'm sure I'll get the hang of it, though." Chris nodded to her and smiled. Darla closed her eyes briefly, saying, "Chris, when I changed, I was overwhelmed by these—"

"Visions? Voices? I had to suffer them as well. It ended with these eyes."

"Oh God, yes, those eyes. Something about them just made me terrified. It was like my fear factor overloaded and I collapsed."

"I know. I don't really understand them, but all those things we saw and heard, I think, are in the other world. Well, anyways, now that we have our other magic caster, we can begin work on getting to that home world. Of course, this will be a rather difficult task. I do believe that the best way to start would be by researching at that man's store. I think it's still up on the strip." He turned to Donnie and Caitlyn. "Do you think you'd be able to do that?" They nodded.

Suddenly, Donnie remembered something. "Hey! I forgot! When we came here, we found Darla's dad wounded! Could that have happened anywhere else?"

Chris thought for a second then said. "It is possible. All around the world, I'm sure there are people who were in the process of dying or hurting. I would assume it was just the nature of Darla's spell that allowed her to transcend my own to save her father. Maybe it was even meant to happen. Who knows?"

"Well, at least those people won't die," said Caitlyn, seeing a hopeful side. "Anyway, should we get going?"

"Yes. I'll send you guys on to the store. Look around a bit and see if you can find anything that will be of use to us." They nodded and stood. Chris lifted a hand and sent them on their way.

He lowered his hand as soon as they were gone and turned to Darla. "All righty. Let's get to work." She nodded and stood as well. Chris walked over to her and stood beside her. "First things first. I want you to learn how to call the tome to you. First, reach up your hand as if you were going to pull a book down from a shelf." She did as such. "Now, think about the tome in your mind and imagine it being the book you are trying to take." She closed her eyes and began to focus on the ancient book. "Now, reach up and take it." She reached into the air and pulled the tome from it. Opening her eyes, she saw nothing there.

"Aw, it didn't work."

Chris chuckled and put an arm around her. "Come on, you can do it. I had to practice a couple of times last night, and all I had to go on were the confounding instructions in the book. Focus a bit harder." She closed her eyes again and reached up in one fluid motion to grab the book. Opening her eyes, she saw that it was beginning to materialize in between her fingers. A small ivory shimmer appeared there but began to fade. She released it and focused her attention harder again. With a confident gesture, she reached into the air. The faint ivory shimmer appeared once more and suddenly faded away, this time leaving an old tome in its place.

She chuckled and looked to Chris with a matter-of-fact grin. "That wasn't so hard."

"This place is just a big mess," exclaimed Caitlyn as she opened up a box and started to go through the contents. Donnie walked about in the dark, dank, and terribly dust-ridden shop. There were large and small cardboard boxes in several stacks around the room, most likely holding the former residents of the now empty shelves. In fact, the only thing in the room that appeared to be relatively recent was the assortment of cobwebs in the corners and inside the counters. A spider was still spinning her web in the corner nearest the boarded door.

Taking note of that boarded door, Caitlyn walked over to it and examined the frame. *How odd*, she thought. *This door should open to the inside and yet the boards are nailed over this side of the door.*

"Kind of strange how everything is still here. I mean, why would the guy close down his store and just leave everything here in boxes? There's enough dust in this place that I'd say no one has been in here for years," Donnie remarked.

Caitlyn turned around and opened another box, pulling out a few books and flipping through them. "I don't think there will be anything in here of use," Caitlyn sighed.

Donnie picked up a few pieces of jewelry that was stored in a small box. "Hey, come here, Catie." She walked over and looked at the jewelry. "Doesn't that look like the same material and design as Darla's bracelet?"

She nodded as she compared the two mentally. "Hmm. That must be where he got it." Donnie put a few of the pieces in his pocket, saying, "Nobody's going to miss these anyway," and continued to look about.

Caitlyn walked over to the counter and looked over it. The glass of the display case had cracked, but dusting it off, she saw nothing inside. She noticed, though, that there was no cash register. On top of the counter, however, was a place where the wood beneath the dust looked a bit less faded and four holes were drilled to outline the corners of a square. Two of the bolts were still partially in the holes though somewhat bent. *Hmm. He must have taken it with him*, she thought.

Donnie was rummaging through some boxes next to the window, not caring how much noise he made. Most of what he was finding at this point included candles, incense, and various burners and holders. "Junk, junk, and more junk. Who would buy this crap anyway?"

Caitlyn laughed a bit and walked behind the counter, opening a door to the back. "Hey, Donnie, do you think this was the room Chris went into?"

Donnie shrugged and joined her at the doorway. "Shall we go inside? Ladies first."

"Oh, thank you, sweet gentleman." She rolled her eyes and walked inside.

In the small room at the back were a large number of empty display cases, cardboard boxes, and bookshelves. They walked around a bit. There was a large box standing in the center of the room. Something was strange about the little room, though. They couldn't quite place it. Donnie suddenly realized. "Caitlyn, look around. Notice something missing? The dust! It totally covered everything out there, but there isn't anything the least bit dusty in here."

Caitlyn looked around and stated an agreement. "This is really odd. Well, Don, let's look through some of this stuff."

Chris pointed to a drawing on one of the pages. "See, that's the Temple of Agape, meaning godly love. It is the most holy place for your kind."

Darla looked over the rather palace-like temple, set beautifully among mountains. "I sense a kind of connection with it from just looking at the picture. It's cool." She smiled and continued flipping pages, each page seeming to bond itself within her mind, like a photographic memory. The two of them were sitting in Chris's living room, thinking a change was needed.

Chris sipped a glass of tea and continued to point out things to her. "I read through this entire book last night. I could probably recite it to you ninety percent correctly. Of course, you will learn it well, too. Well, I think we need to contact the others. Let's see here." He flipped a few pages and read over a spell called "Window," then stood up and walked to his bathroom, turning on the light but not shutting the door. He touched the mirror and ripples started to shimmer through it, the reflection disappearing and turning into a window-like scene of the store that the other two were now exploring. "Hey, how are you two faring? Find anything interesting yet?"

"Is that you? Chris?"

He chuckled at the sound of Caitlyn's voice. "Yeah, it's me! Look for a mirror or some kind of reflective surface. I'm looking at what appears to be a boarded up window and a door." He waited as he saw Donnie and Caitlyn step into view.

Caitlyn looked at the image for a minute then said, "Why are you on the counter's display case window?"

Chris chuckled. "Just needed to talk to you. Find anything yet?"

Donnie nodded his head, saying, "Yeah. I got some really expensive looking jewelry that may come in handy. We also found this room in the back. It's the one you were talking about. It is pretty much empty, save some junk in a few old boxes, a few books we found, and, oh, inside this tall box was a great big pedestal with a large ball on it. It shocked me when I touched it, so I think it might be the one you touched."

Chris nodded. "All right, do you need any more time to look around?" Caitlyn shook her head. "All right. I'll call you guys back. Stand beside the pedestal. I'm going to bring it back with you as well. It might prove to be more than just a static electricity magnet." They nodded and disappeared from sight. Chris heard the faint call of "ready" from Donnie and touched the mirror again, dispelling the image from it. He walked back to the living room. Darla was still there, pawing through the spell book.

"Would you care to call them back here? Try and read that spell from the tome. It may only work for me." Darla nodded and flipped through the book a bit, reading over a page then lifting her hand, making a bright white shower of sparkling light fall from the ceiling.

When it disappeared, Donnie and Caitlyn appeared with the pedestal. Donnie held in his hands three large books.

"All right, let's get started on these books. Darla and I will most likely be the only ones that can read them, so I want you two to examine this pedestal. See if there is anything odd about it." Donnie and Caitlyn nodded to Chris and started to work on their task. Chris picked up the stack of books and carried them into the kitchen, setting them on the table. Darla followed and sat down, taking the top book from the stack and beginning to flip through it. Chris took one as well and began to read.

A few hours later, they didn't have very much accomplished along the lines of getting them across the two worlds. Caitlyn and Donnie discovered that the ball could not be removed from the stand by physical means. It couldn't be moved by any magical mean either, as Chris found. Darla and Chris didn't find out very much about how to get to their home world. After having looked through the first book, it was found to be of a fictional literature basis. Apparently, there were poets and authors in the other world. The second book was filled with historical documents on the kings, wars, and other information irrelevant to their search. Chris picked up the third book, saying, "I'll take this last one. Darla, could you fix us a bite to eat? Get Caitlyn to help. You can search the cabinets and fridge." Darla nodded and stood up, walking to Caitlyn and Donnie who were lounging about in the living room. Donnie was playing a video game since the TV wouldn't work without someone to run the cable stations. Caitlyn was reading a regular book.

"Catie, can you give me a hand in here? I think we ought to fix something to eat." She nodded and stood up, setting her book down and walking to Darla.

Donnie perked up at the mention of food and said, "Hey, why don't we just order a pizza?" The two girls gave him a strange look for a second, but then he caught himself. "Oh, yeah, right. No delivery guys."

Chris flipped through the last book slowly, becoming rather hungry at the smell of the food the girls were cooking. He walked into the kitchen, seeing some chicken in a fryer on one counter, a couple of pots on the stove, and a pan of rolls in the oven. "This looks really good, girls."

Caitlyn smiled to Darla, putting another pot on the stove. "Bet you didn't know we could cook, did you Chris?" He chuckled and shook his head. "Darla had to do some mumbo jumbo to get the stove to work, though," she said, stirring the contents of her pot.

"Yeah, I had to do the same with the TV and the video game. I guess without workers, electricity doesn't work. Though exactly why the tome had a spell for such a situation, I'm not sure."

Caitlyn nodded and looked towards the living room, calling, "Donnie, come on! Dinner's almost ready."

"I'm almost done; just have to beat this last boss!"

"Well, don't be too long," called Darla, starting to toss a salad.

"Yeah, Don, I'm hungry too and I don't want you holding up my stomach," shouted Chris. He walked over to the pots, seeing mashed potatoes, a bit of macaroni and cheese, and green beans.

After they had finished their meal, the four of them sat at the table, sipping soft drinks and having a conversation. Chris was still reading his book.

"What's taking you so long, Chris? The girls cooked us a great meal and you haven't taken your eyes off that book for a second, even while you were eating," said Donnie.

Chris looked to him and sighed. "Well, this one is rather large in and of itself and the dialect of the language is a bit different from the others. I do think I may be on to something, though."

He returned to reading as Donnie turned to Darla and Caitlyn.

"Well, I must say, you two did an excellent job on the meal, even if you did cook too much." Caitlyn looked at him with a grin on her face and nodded a thank you.

Darla looked at him and playfully scoffed. "Cooked too much? Look at you! There isn't a piece of food left on the table thanks to Mr. Second-Helpings here and you say we cooked too much?"

They all laughed as Donnie took another sip of his drink then said, "Well, maybe it wasn't *too* much."

"We'll try not to disappoint with breakfast tomorrow," said Caitlyn.

"In the intric flow cycle, the transport chamber will form from catalysts light and energy," Chris said, reading partially aloud, partially to himself.

"What is it?" Darla asked him.

"Well, it seems to be telling me how exactly the pedestal works as far as creating the link between this world and the other one, but how we get that link linked isn't exactly clear."

"I'm certain you'll get it soon," said Caitlyn. She stood up and began clearing plates from the table. Donnie stood to help her.

"Have you seen any kind of spells or incantations that might be relevant?" asked Darla.

"Not really. This thing reads more like a computer manual than a magic book. It seems like it's all—wait, here it is!"

"What? Have you found something?"

"Yes, this is the incantation! Come with me!"

He stood up and walked into the living room, laughing a bit. He stood beside the pedestal and waited for them all to join him, which they did rather quickly. "It's very simple. This pedestal opens the gateway to our world. All we have to do is say this simple incantation, place one hand on the pedestal, and join our other hands over top of it."

They looked at him and smiled. "Good job, Chris," Caitlyn remarked.

45

"All right. I think we ought to get a good night's sleep before we go," Darla said, looking out one of the windows to see the darkness of the night. They hadn't realized so much time had passed. Everyone agreed with her.

"Well, let's see here. You girls can take the den. It's the largest room in the house and, since my uncle uses it for his bedroom whenever he's home, it's got the largest bed. Donnie and I will take my room. We've got the bunk beds so we'll be fine." They all agreed on the plan. A little bit later, they decided to retire for the night.

Both pairs hadn't gone to sleep yet, even at midnight. They stayed up, each sitting and talking to each other. Chris looked through his closet once more, having found that the clothing was now gone and exchanged with several sorcerers' robes, tunics, pants, and other articles. He assumed that they had been replaced at the metamorphosis and confirmed it as Darla's closet was found to be full of clerical robes, blouses, pants, etc.

Around one in the morning, the guys had finally gotten ready to go to sleep when they heard a knock at the door. Chris got up and walked over, opening the door. Darla stood there in a light robe. A nightshirt and pajama bottoms she had borrowed from Caitlyn could be seen underneath. "I can't sleep. Catie has already knocked off and I have no one to talk to. Would you like to go outside for a bit and talk?"

Chris, standing in only his light pants, nodded, saying, "Sure. Let me get a robe and house shoes on and I'll come right out." Darla nodded and walked down the hall. Chris slipped his shoes on and wrapped a sheer robe about him, walking to the door.

He was stopped by the sound of Donnie's voice. "Have her in by curfew, young man. Don't want to catch you sneaking in."

Chris chuckled. "Thanks, Dad. Can I borrow your car and twenty bucks?" They both laughed and Chris walked out, closing the door behind him.

He walked down the hall and to the back door, stepping out onto the deck, feeling the cool night air hit him nicely. He walked over to the hammock where she was sitting, putting one hand on the stand to brace himself as he hopped up into it. He looked up into the night sky, seeing all the stars and sighed a bit. "So, what's on your mind, Darla?" She remained silent for a while, watching the sky as well. "Nothing really. I just wanted to enjoy the stars with someone." They both smiled and rocked back and forth in the hammock. Darla scooted down a bit, laying back, just watching the stars.

Chris looked to her, saying, "It is very nice out here, don't you think?"

"Yeah. It's even better with you." He smiled to her, lying back as well. Darla edged a bit closer to him, resting her head against his chest. "I feel different here with you, Chris. There is a connection between us that wasn't there before. I feel so much safer with you, even though I know there isn't anything on this world that can harm me anymore." He nodded a bit as she continued to talk. "I don't know. Maybe it's the way we have changed. It's as if we gained five or ten years all of a sudden. We're no longer like immature teenagers, more like young adults." He chuckled a bit and sighed.

"Then again, you never were really an immature teenager." She turned to look at him. "There was always something about you that told me you weren't like the rest of them. You always did have more maturity. More wisdom. Was it all magic?"

He shook his head a bit. "Don't know, really. I do seem to have blossomed a bit, though."

"Yeah. I became a young woman and you became a young man. Will Donnie and Caitlyn change too?" Chris nodded. Darla sighed a bit. "Hmm. I wonder what they will become."

"Well, I know your change didn't affect you much. You were always fantastic both on the outside and on the inside. I'm glad I changed. I may have had the personality going for me, but at least now I look a whole lot better."

Darla chuckled a bit. "You always did have nice eyes though." Chris smiled and continued to watch the stars.

Darla's eyes lingered on him for a bit then turned to the sky again.

The two of them continued to talk for a long time. It was as if they were discovering each other for the first time, even though they had known each other for so long.

Chris raised his hand and twisted his wrist, a small blanket dropping onto them from the air near his hand.

After a couple hours, Darla's eyes began to slowly droop down, though, and soon she was fast asleep. Chris looked at her, wrapping an arm around her to keep her a bit warmer and watched her as she slept.

His eyes remained on her until the sun crested the hill behind his house.

4

Homecoming

Around eight or so in the morning, Darla woke up. Stretching out a bit then sitting up, she noticed Chris sleeping beside her. *I wonder how long he was awake last night?* she thought. She nudged his shoulder gently, rousing him from his sleep.

"Hmm…oh…no school today…sleep late…"

Darla chuckled a bit and shook him a bit harder. "Wake up, you sleepyhead!" He opened his eyes, looking to her softly, and then reached up to rub the sleep from his eyes. "How long did you stay awake last night?"

He smiled softly, sitting up a bit. "Oh, not very long after you went to sleep. I kept watch over you until about sunrise."

She blushed slightly, smiling. "Oh, you didn't have to do that. I don't think anything would have gotten me. Besides, you only got maybe two or three hours of sleep, Chris."

He chuckled, saying, "Don't worry about me. I'll be quite all right. I am a light sleeper anyways. I never get more than six hours a night. What, think I was going to take advantage of you in your sleep?" She laughed and grabbed the pillow from the hammock, smacking him against the head. Caught off guard, he tried to roll out of the way, unfortunately causing the hammock to flip, sending both of them in the blanket to the wooden deck.

They laughed a bit as they tried to pick themselves up. "Oh, you goof! Look what you did!" Darla laughed.

49

"Me? You're the one that hit me with a pillow!"

After getting themselves together, they went inside to get ready for the day. Chris walked to the bathroom where Donnie was already brushing his teeth. Donnie attempted to ask him why he did not come in last night. However, with a mouth full of toothpaste foam, it was rather hard to understand.

"Didn't your mom teach you not to talk with your mouth full?" Donnie chuckled and spit into the sink, grabbing the bottle of mouthwash and pouring a bit in his mouth, starting to gargle. The tone of it wavered a bit as Donnie tried to continue to speak. Chris looked at him with a strange look, grabbing his electric razor and beginning to shave. "Seeing as how this conversation has taken a drastic turn for the worst, I'll have to rescue it." He stretched out his neck and continued to shave. "Darla and I just sat out on the hammock and talked. Nothing special."

Donnie spit into the sink, turning on the water to rinse it down. "Oh really? Then why didn't you come back in when you were done?"

Chris laughed a bit. "Well, we didn't really get done. We talked for quite a long time. She fell asleep and I watched her for a while then went to sleep myself. Then we woke up. No big deal."

Donnie chuckled to himself and shook his head. "Sure Romeo. No big deal." Chris laughed and punched him in the shoulder. "Ouch! Hey, that actually hurt! A hit from Chris actually hurt. I never thought I'd see the day…"

Chris smirked at him then walked over to the shower, turning on the water. "You already had your shower, right? Well, finish up and let me get mine." Donnie frowned in a mock complaint and grabbed a comb, walking out and shutting the door behind him.

Darla stepped into the guest bathroom and turned on the water in the shower. Letting it get just warm enough, she walked to a shelf and chose a towel. All of a sudden, she heard a knock at the door. Walking over to it, she opened it to find Caitlyn standing there. "Oh, I'm sorry, Darla. I didn't know you were getting ready to take a shower."

"No problem, Catie. What do you need?"

"Oh, I just wanted to get my hair bands. I left them in here after my shower."

"You've already had yours?"

"Yeah, I got up early and took my shower. I always get up with the sunrise." Darla nodded as Caitlyn reached over and grabbed her bands. "So, where were you off to last night? I woke up a couple of times during the night and you weren't in bed."

Darla placed her towel on the rack just outside the shower door and walked over to grab a washcloth. "Oh, nowhere really, I just went to lie outside in the hammock."

"Oh? By yourself?"

"No...with Chris..."

"Oh?" Caitlyn grinned. "Darla, you little she-devil."

Darla laughed, shaking her head. "It was nothing like that. We just talked." She sighed. "He was really sweet, though. He just listened to my voice like it was the only thing in the world he wanted to hear." Darla turned to the shower again.

Caitlyn frowned a bit after Darla's eyes had passed her. "How wonderful. You two might make a cute couple."

"Mm-hmm. Yeah. Sure." She chuckled scoffingly, though in her mind she secretly smiled to herself. "Anyways, you've got your bands, now go. I'd like to have a little privacy for my shower." Caitlyn laughed and walked out, pulling the door shut behind her.

After everyone had done their morning routine and had breakfast, Chris took Donnie and Darla took Caitlyn to their respective houses to pack. They were allowed one bag each, but Chris made the suggestion that they use backpacks. Chris took out a few slips of paper from his pocket. "All right, everyone. I've copied down the incantation for everyone to use. I've written it so that you can sound it out and get pretty close. I don't think it has to be exact as long as one or two of us can say it correctly." They nodded to Chris, taking their slips from him.

"Is everyone ready?" Chris asked. They all nodded and put their packs on. Within them were a few changes of clothes, some food, and other little things. Chris's bag made a slight jingling sound from the collection of gold, jewelry, and coins he had asked them all to bring so that they would possibly have something considered valuable for trade.

He stretched out his hand above the gateway pedestal and placed his other on the side of the orb. They each in turn did the same, linking hands over the top. Chris began the chant, the others beginning to follow as well. As the words became louder and louder, the ball began to glow. A blanket of dark clouds rolled over the sky above the house as their chanting grew. The electricity flowing through the ball became stronger and stronger, flowing through their bodies. Suddenly, the globe began to change color. Shapes began to become visible on the surface. It was as if it were turning into a real globe. The outline of two continents began to form on its surface, color filling in the shapes in bright greens, blues and browns. They continued to chant, the glow of the globe intensifying, beginning to pulse out from within it, filling the room. A sound of rushing wind filled the house as the glow spread over the four bodies, completely coating them. As it grew in intensity, they had to avert their eyes as it became almost blinding.

Suddenly, with a quick flash, the whole house rumbled, then the wind stopped, the glow died down, the color faded from the orb, and the chanting fell away. Light returned to the skies, shining in the windows of the living room. Yet, no one was there to cast a shadow.

* * *

With a yawn, and a slight groan, Chris slowly started to awaken. The sky above him was a beautiful shade of blue, specked with just a few white, puffy clouds. There was a bright sun shining, and beyond that, the outline of two moons, one slightly larger than the other. There was a light breeze blowing, and it gave the air a bit of a chill, like a mid-autumn air.

Chris sat up a bit more, his eyes opening fully. He found himself lying on a green hill overlooking a small ocean town, people walking about the streets, and several ships in the harbor. It was by no means a large town, no more than twenty homes, a few larger buildings, and a small marketplace, but it obviously was a port city. Beyond the docks, he could see a beautiful ocean spanning the horizon. "It's...amazing..."

Caitlyn was the next to rise, slowly sitting up. She looked at to Chris for a moment, looked at the other two, then back to Chris, following his gaze out to the beautiful sight. Donnie and Darla soon woke up as well, eventually making it to a sitting position, but they, too, couldn't help but stare at their surroundings.

Judging by the sun, Chris assumed that if the sun's position was the same in both worlds, they were looking west over the ocean. To the north, you could see miles and miles of valleys and fields, set off by a range of mountains off in the distance. Behind them, the mountains swung around a bit closer, and now were just a mile or two away. To the south was a small, green pasture, dotted with trees that grew consistently in number until they formed a great forest no more than five or six hundred yards away.

It was truly amazing. They had never seen such pure beauty in all their lives. Earth had become so overrun with buildings and cars and technology that it was too easy to become completely lost from the beauty of nature. Now, it completely surrounded them.

Donnie was the first to speak. "It's so beautiful, but I thought there was supposed to be a darkness covering this land."

Chris looked at him, noticing the same, yet shrugging. "I don't really know. This place is obviously too beautiful to be infected with the darkness."

They others nodded a bit and continued to glance around in awe. "Well, we appear to have everything," Darla said, looking over their packs. "So we ought to go look around that town."

"Wait a sec, guys. What about Donnie and me? If we couldn't read this place's language, we might not be able to speak it," said Catie. Donnie agreed.

"Well, I'm not exactly sure what is going to happen. Darla and I talked about this earlier. When we look at words in the new language, they just seem to slide into our heads as English. Almost as if our brain translates them as we go. Let me try speaking a bit of it to you," Chris said. "Let's see. All right, see if you understand this. Hello, sir. How are you today?"

"Thought you were going to speak in the other language," remarked Donnie, not hearing any difference.

"I was speaking it. Try this. Go over to the chair."

"Go over to the chair. You're speaking English," said Caitlyn.

"No, I'm speaking in the other language. Very strange. We'll see, though, if it works with locals."

Darla was first to spot the Kelara Bay Inn lying on the main road. They walked inside and took a look around. Chris motioned over to the adjacent tavern and the four walked over, setting their stuff down at a table near the back. He and Donnie walked over to the bar and motioned the tender over.

"Excuse...me...sir...can...we...get...two...rooms?" Donnie asked the man, very slowly and quite enunciated.

"What's the matter, boy? I can understand you just fine. Don't you speak Syerican? Ain't no other language around, so unless you're spouting gibberish at me, you've got to be speaking my way."

"Oh, I'm sorry, sir. I—come from a place that doesn't speak Syerican."

"Where's that at, son? Nearly everyone on the two continents speaks it!"

It was very strange, but in the young man's mind, the words sounded just like regular English. He could almost pick up what would have been an American southern accent!

"Um, never mind. It's not important," interrupted Chris. "Can we get two rooms?"

"How long do you want 'em for?" the man asked with a rather agitated attitude.

"About a week, I would guess."

"That'll run you a lot of coin. Sure you're gonna stay that long?"

"Well, we don't exactly have any money on us. We're…uh…just passing through and needed to stop. We're—I'm a trader. I deal in jewelry and I…just bought a whole inventory. I could trade you, say, this?" Chris pulled out a gold, jeweled pocket watch Caitlyn had brought along. It had been an anniversary gift from her mother to her father. Donnie walked over to the table where Caitlyn and Darla sat.

"Well, that's a pretty nice trinket you got there. You give me that there watch and you've got a room and meals while you're here."

"Works for me. Here you go," said Chris, handing him the watch. The man took it, looking it over with a great smile, knowing he could get a nice bit of gold for it. He walked over to a key rack on the wall and took two adjacent brass keys. "The rooms are upstairs, side by side."

"Thank you, sir. Oh, and can I get a pitcher of ale?" The man nodded, filling one from a barrel tap and setting it on a tray with mugs. Chris took it and walked over to the table.

"It looks like the town is just fine. No one seems to be any weaker or sicker than the next person," Donnie commented, noticing Chris's approach. "Do you think there will be anyone here who would be able to give us any leads, Chris?"

Chris shrugged, saying, "I don't really know. There might be a lord or something of that nature. If anyone would have the info, it might be him." He sat the tray down and poured each person a mug of ale. "It may not be safe to walk around town by ourselves, so we'll split up. After we get rested up a bit," Chris said, turning to Caitlyn, "you and I will go talk to whoever runs this place. Darla, Donnie, why don't you two explore the town? Get a feel for things, and talk to some people." They nodded to him and drank from their mugs.

After they were done, they parted and walked through the town. Chris and Caitlyn headed down the main road of the town, glancing around for anything that might resemble a town hall. Caitlyn spotted a semi-formal looking building and the two headed towards it. Stepping in, she noticed a rather old-looking woman sitting at a desk to the side. "Excuse me, miss? Could you tell us if this is the town hall?"

55

The woman nodded, yet chuckled a bit, saying, "Sure is, missy, but if you're wantin' to speak to the mayor, you're out of luck. He ain't here. Generally don't show up around here most of the time. He lives in a big old mansion out in the woods beyond Gammeron Plains and doesn't come 'round here but on tax day."

Chris sighed a bit, nodding. "Would we be able to get out there to see him?"

She shook her head, saying, "I doubt it. He's got a bunch of big thugs hanging around the place. No one gets in but someone with couple of shiny coins to donate into his hands, if you catch my drift." She chuckled a bit and leaned back in her chair. "Sorry, kids."

Darla and Donnie had seen the general store, the vegetable market, and the jail. They'd talked to a lot of shopkeepers and townspeople. They passed the post office, noticing the sign that said it would be closed for the weekend. They also saw a church that had a few people in it, thus they assumed it was some equivalent to Sunday. This seemed like a perfectly normal town. The people gave them a few strange looks, however, as they noticed well that Donnie didn't fit in. His jeans, t-shirt, and sneakers didn't quite fit with the tunic and twill fashion style of these people. As the sky started to lose a bit of its blue to a soft orange, the two found themselves walking down the main road aimlessly.

"I think we should just go on back to the tavern and wait for the other two," Darla said.

"Yeah, that might be a good idea. I don't think we're going to find anything here," Donnie replied. Suddenly, a tall, burly man stepped into his way, causing Donnie to bump into him.

The man looked down at him, saying, "Excuse me, kid, but what do you think you're doing, running into people?"

Donnie looked the rather brute looking man over and said, "I didn't mean to...you just popped up out of nowhere...I..."

The man looked over at Darla, eyeing her for a bit, then turned back to Donnie. "Look, kid, you just better watch where you're going. Not everyone in the world is as friendly as me." He pushed

Donnie aside and walked past him, reaching back to pinch Darla's posterior as he passed.

She flung around, rather angrily, and pulled her hands up into fists, saying, "You shouldn't..."

Donnie grabbed her hands and shook his head. "Now is not the time to make enemies. Just ignore him. Once we leave this town, we won't have to put up with him anymore. Besides, we probably won't see him again anyways." The man chuckled to himself as he continued to walk away.

She nodded and lowered her hands, grumbling foul things under her breath. The two of them continued walking.

Chris and Caitlyn had already returned to the tavern and were sitting and talking when the door opened. From the silhouettes placed against the sunset orange sky, they could tell it was Darla and Donnie. "Well, did you find anything interesting?" Chris asked.

Darla shook her head, saying, "Nothing. Seems to be a rather plain town. I don't think we're going to find any clues here."

Caitlyn shook her head. "I don't think so either. I think the thing to do might be to go see that mayor." She filled the other two in on what they had learned from the old lady.

Donnie arched a brow, saying, "Hmm. A recluse. Well, he may know something. We'll try him tomorrow."

"Yes, but for now, we'll hang here for the rest of the night and see what we can do tomorrow," said Chris. The other two nodded and they continued to talk for a while as the sun continued its drop. The tender stepped out from behind the bar and began to light some small oil lanterns hung from the ceiling in various places around the room, finishing the last just as the final remnants of light faded outside.

5

Small Town

At the crack of dawn, a rooster began to crow just a few yards down from the inn as it sat atop the fence of one of the townspersons. Awakened by the sound, Chris rose out of bed and began to get dressed. As he pulled on a pair of dark brown pants and a green tunic, a bit of clothing he discovered in his home-world closet, he walked over and shook Donnie's shoulder gently. He reluctantly woke up and began to stretch a bit, eventually following Chris in getting dressed, donning a solid blue t-shirt and jeans. A wind blew in through the window and the chill of the morning air made Chris grab his robe and wrap it about his back. He fastened it at the neck, leaving the hood down and the front open for now. He loosely tied the belt. The two of them walked together down to the tavern and, smelling the fresh coffee, ordered four mugs, taking a seat at a table. Apparently, not everything was completely different between this world and the other.

Caitlyn and Darla were soon spotted coming down the stairs, Caitlyn was dressed in a very simple blouse and jeans. Darla was dressed in a white cloak, golden silk trimming the neck and shoulders, with a light blue pair of pants and a white blouse on under it. They walked over to the table and took a cup of coffee each, taking sips to help wake them up.

Donnie yawned and said, "Well, it certainly is a lovely morning. Not too hot, not too cold. They have great weather, for a darkness-infested doomed planet."

With a chuckle, Caitlyn nodded, saying, "Yes, but it certainly was a change not waking up to a loud alarm clock."

"What's on the agenda for today, Chris?" Darla asked.

"Well, I think we ought to just do a bit of mixing around in the town. Talk to some residents; see what there is to do here, etc. I think I can get us a little bit of money. I noticed a house that had a roof about to cave in. I might be able to fix it with magic, for a nominal fee, of course. I saw a guy pay the tender in gold coins here, yesterday, so I figure that's the currency they use."

"That's a good idea. There's a post office in town. Darla and I saw it yesterday. I think I may go back there today, if it's open, and see if they have any kind of maps or something like that," said Donnie. "I'll take a bit of paper and jot some notes if I see anything noteworthy."

Darla and Caitlyn looked to each other for a second, then Darla said, "We're going shopping. We'll see if we can find anything useful."

Chris nodded and reached into his pocket, drawing out a few pieces of jewelry and setting them on the table. "Watch some of the people around here as they do their trading, then try to figure up the value of this stuff from what you learn. Try and trade it for coins first, and try not to get ripped off."

The two girls nodded and Caitlyn took the jewelry, placing it in her pocket, and saying, "Well, let's get a bit of breakfast, shall we?"

After the meal, the four sat talking for another couple of hours. They figured there would be no point in leaving too early as the marketplace probably wouldn't be in full swing right that early, nor would they wish to wake the people living in the leaky-roofed house. An hour or so before noon, they departed.

Chris walked down the main street, glancing to and fro at the locals, waving and smiling to each. He wanted to make a good impression, as they could no doubt sense that he was a stranger in the town. He looked about for the house he had spotted yesterday, turning a corner and spotting the little place down the block a bit. He stopped and waved the tome into his hand. He flipped it open, looking through it to see if he had a repair spell written in. As he flipped through it, he noticed that he didn't have any spells in it at all! The spells he cast before they came over were totally gone. He assumed that the travel through the gateway must have caused it. It also meant that all of Darla's spells were gone as well. With a sigh, he waved the tome away and made a mental note to alert the others to this.

He walked toward it and saw that a small hole had appeared in the roof since yesterday. There was a man, seeming about in his fifties or so, sitting on the covered porch of the small cottage, seeming to be deeply engrossed in thought. He walked up to the porch, knocking on one of the posts that supported the overhang. The man snapped out of his thought and looked to Chris, saying, "Something I can do for you, young man?"

Chris smiled and shook his head, saying, "Actually, there is something I may be able to do for you. My name is Chris. I couldn't help but notice your roof problem."

The man sighed and nodded, "Yeah. The thing's about to give way. I just don't have the gold to get it fixed. M' name is Richard. I'd assume you're a traveler, yes?"

"Something along that line, yes."

"Yeah, well, the town carpenter, Hellard, sold me these repair spells here." He reached into his pocket and pulled out two small brown orbs. "But he won't use it on m' roof for less than a hundred piece. I just don't make that from the bread shop."

"You own a bakery?"

"Yeah, me and my wife. She's over there now. I don't bring in near that much to spare, though, not even in the travel seasons."

Chris smiled and walked up to him, saying, "What if I told you I might be willing to fix it, for, say, seventy gold, and that I could have it done by sunset?"

The man looked up, arching a brow. "Seventy gold? You mean you can use one of these things?"

"Yes. It just so happens that I am a traveling mage. Me and a group of my friends, four of us together, are here just passing through and we need a bit of gold for provisions."

"Hmm. We ain't had a mage in this town in a few months. I'll tell you what. I'll go fifty gold, I'll give you the other orb, and dinner for the four of you at the bakery."

"Sir, you've got yourself a deal." Chris extended his hand and Richard took it, giving it a firm shake with a grin. "I'll get started right away."

The man handed Chris the two orbs with a smile. Chris took them and walked to the front of the house, raising one of them between his hands toward the roof and beginning a small chant. As the orb began to glow, the man smiled and walked out to view his work.

Darla and Caitlyn were browsing the various little shops and carts in the marketplace. The very large, circular shape and central location gave the impression that it served the function of a town square, albeit the wrong shape. This was further aided in that it looked like most of the townspersons did their commerce here, as well as their conversation. Several women were sitting on one of the wooden benches that were set beside a great tree in the center of the circle. A few young children were playing off to one side while their parents did their shopping or selling. After studying the various transactions going on between the villagers and the salesmen, they roughly figured a trade rate of prices and began to looks for a good trader for their jewelry. They spotted a rather large cart that had several articles of clothing hanging on its sides and front, and various pieces of apparel on stands in front of the cart. Darla noticed a few pieces of metalwork lying on top of the counter of the cart to one side.

Caitlyn took a piece from her pocket and handed it to Darla. With a nod, she placed it in her own pocket and walked up to the counter, noticing a bit of rather plain jewelry and accessories lying atop the wood of the countertop to the opposite side of the metal pieces. The man sitting behind it was counting some gold coins and hardly noticed her arrival. "See anything you like, lass?"

"We're just browsing a bit, sir, but I do believe you might be able to help me." She took out a diamond pendant on a long gold chain and a thin bracelet speckled in various gemstones and placed them on the counter. The man jumped up and leaned over, looking them over.

"Now those are mighty fine pieces you have there."

"I know. However, they could become yours should the price be right."

Caitlyn smiled at Darla's smooth talk as she picked up a hat and tried it on. She put it down and continued to look over the things on the stands.

"Hmm. Let me see," the man replied as he took the pendant in his hands, looking it over. He set it down and picked up the bracelet, examining it as well. Then, he looked up and began to peer at the two girls, noticing that he hadn't seen them before. *Travelers*, he thought. *Might not know the exchange rate.* He cleared his throat and said, "Well, you see, the jewel on the pendant's got this little scratch right there and the bracelet, why, those gems don't even look real. I'd say that drops their value down to…a hundred twenty gold?"

Darla laughed and looked at the man. "One hundred twenty gold? What do you take me for, a fool? That pendant is worth no less than one hundred fifty gold. The bracelet has got to be worth the majority of that as well."

"A hundred fifty, surely not—a hundred thirty, perhaps."

"One hundred forty-five." She peered at him with a woman's cunning.

"One forty and ninety for the bracelet."

"Sold," Darla exclaimed with a bright smile. The man leaned over to what Darla assumed to be a locked box hidden behind the counter, taking a key from his pocket and unlocking it, removing from within the gold. He placed it on the counter and took the jewelry, grinning as he placed them in the safe. They were obviously pieces of a higher worth than most of the other stuff he had traded before.

Darla took the gold, counting one large coin and thirteen coins of a bit smaller size.

"It's all there, missy. A hundred piece and thirteen ten pieces. Anything else I can get you? Perhaps a nice pouch to put that in?"

She thought for a bit and nodded. "Something light, but versatile."

The man nodded and walked over to a small box on one table, fiddling through it a bit and pulling out a small, brown, drawstring belt pouch. "Here you go. It's made of a strong cloth, so it shouldn't rip or tear, and I'll tell you what, I'll let you have it for free." He handed it to her with a smile.

"Thank you, sir." She took the pouch and put the coins inside, placing the pouch in her pocket. She turned around and walked to Caitlyn who was looking at a cloak on the side of the stand. It was a light violet with various spots of gold and green trim. It appeared to be just a bit taller than Caitlyn was, but she was still taken with it anyways.

Caitlyn grinned as Darla approached. "Very nice work. See what you can get this for."

She nodded and walked back over to the man. "My friend here needs a new cloak."

The man looked at the girl, noticing that she was dressed in a very strange manner of clothing. "Well, that's a fine cloak there. Lined in fine Carhath wool. Got that from a trader who passed through here not five days ago. Sold it to me for fifty gold. I think I might be willing to let it go for—say—forty?"

Darla walked over to the cloak and examined the inside and, noting that the man had already been pulling some tricks, decided to take a chance. "Well, you see, I was just in Carhath a few weeks ago, and their wool is much thicker than this."

The man looked to her with a rather aggravated sigh, saying, "All right, all right. It's from Terrun. Look, how about you give me twenty for the cloak and skip off before you start turning away my other customers."

"Thirty-five and you throw in this black one over here as well. I know it's nowhere near 'Carhath wool,'" she said with a slight mocking tone.

"Look, missy, I'll have you know—" The man noticed that a woman who came up to look at a hat was turned away by their talk.

He spoke up, saying, "No, no, miss, this is the finest wool in these parts. Why it isn't any—" He got quieter, saying, "Fine! Fine! Give me my gold, take them, and get out of here!"

Darla took the gold from her pouch and handed it to the man. Caitlyn took the violet cloak and wrapped it around her shoulders, grabbing the other one and draping it over her arm.

"Thank you. Let us take our leave and continue looking around." The two stepped away from the cart and continued their walk around the marketplace.

Donnie walked up to the door of the post office, finding the sign that had been there in the window gone and several people walking within the small building. He pushed the door open and walked inside, seeing the postmaster standing behind a long counter, behind which were several small shelves, each sectioned off into squares and marked with names of various townspeople. The last few boxes were slightly larger and had no name, but a bit of assorted letters within. He assumed that those larger boxes were for mail that had no other box to claim.

As he walked over to the counter, he stood in line behind two other people, a young man and a middle-aged woman, the postmaster getting each one their mail from their respective box. Once the postmaster reached Donnie, he smiled, saying, "Hello, stranger. New in town?"

"Yes, I'm just passing through with a few of my friends. I was wondering if you had any kind of maps or something that I might be able to look at."

"Why, yes, sir, I do. What region to you need?"

"Well…I don't really know my way around this area too well, so how about just a map of this region, to start."

The man nodded and walked to one end of the counter, reaching to a shelf beneath and pulling out a stack of papers. After sorting through them for a bit, he brought two over, placing them before Donnie. "Here you go. This here is the Gammeron Plains map and the map for the Coastal Mountains."

With a nod, he took the papers and walked to the other end of the counter to be out of the way, taking a piece of paper from his pocket and a pencil, starting to make rough sketches as he looked over the papers.

The postmaster watched Donnie for a second, wondering what the stick he was using to write with exactly was, but with a shrug, he turned back to his work. At that moment, the sound of horse hooves and rickety wooden wheels became apparent as a carriage pulled up outside. A young man walked in, no more than twenty of age, with a large leather bag hanging from his shoulder.

"Hello there, Wilbur. Got another round of letters for you. Sorry about the delay, but there was a rockslide on the mount and it gave me a bit of trouble. I had to go around it."

Donnie turned to watch as the postmaster smiled at the young man, who then took from his bag a large stack of various shaped letters, the paper looking a bit different than that Donnie had, of course. The deliverer sat them on the counter and the postmaster took from beneath the counter a rather small bag that jingled with the sound of coins, handing it to the young man. With a smile and a nod, the lad took the pouch and placed it in his bag, waving a bit and heading out the door with a, "See you in a few weeks, Wilbur."

The postmaster waved to the lad and started to sort through the letters, going over each one and placing each in its slot. "Hmm. Widow Martin...Brewster...Aleric...McCaffrey..."

Donnie looked back to the maps and continued to write as the man kept saying the names to himself.

"Old John...Geoffries...another for Brewster..."

Donnie switched the maps out and began to take notes on the second.

"Mayor Brickshire...Mrs. Galami...hmm...what's this?"

Donnie continued to write, paying little attention to the man who now puzzled over the name on the letter in his hand.

"Four from Earth. What does that mean?"

Donnie ceased writing, his face turning rather somber as he raised his head, slowly turning it toward the man.

"Hmm...well, I guess I'll just put it in the junk box and see who claims it." He placed the letter in one of the larger boxes at the end and continued putting away the other mail.

"Excuse me, sir, but what did that letter say?"

He looked to Donnie, then reached in and took the letter back out, looking over it and saying, "It was—yes—Four from Earth. Quite cryptic. Why, son, do you know what it means?"

With a slight nod, he walked down the counter to where the man was standing. "Yes. I am—my friends and I—we're from a place called Earth."

"Ah, well, I've never heard of it before." He handed him the letter and went back about his business.

"Thank...you..." Donnie took the letter, looking over the calligraphic letters on the front, turning it over to reveal a wax seal, imprinted with the symbol of the moons. He puzzled over the paper for a while, and then decided that it would be best if he didn't open it until the group met back up. He walked over and took the paper on which he had taken the notes and put it and the letter in his pocket. With an almost frightened countenance, he left the post office and walked back toward the tavern.

"Come again, lad." The postmaster continued to sort the rest of his letters, finishing and walking over to take back up the maps. "Strange young lad, I must say."

6

The Letter

In the early part of the afternoon, Caitlyn and Darla had finished shopping and started to head back to the tavern. As they walked inside, they noticed that no one else had returned yet. In fact, the tavern was rather empty itself. Beyond the bartender, there was no one there at all. They walked over to the bar and ordered a pitcher of water, walking back to their usual table. It wasn't too warm on this cool yet sunny day, but they felt like getting a cool drink.

The tender walked out back of the tavern with a pitcher to a small well pump and pumped it full of crystal clear water. Walking back into the tavern, he reached into a small jar and pulled out a marble-sized blue orb, saying a small chant, and dropping it into the pitcher. Instantly, the orb began to glow and a bit of condensation formed on the outside of the pitcher. He took two glasses and brought them with the pitcher over to their table. The girls poured themselves glasses, finding that the water was very cold, assuming that the orb was to account for that. They chatted for a while as they drank their water.

The roof was now patched and rather solid as Chris dropped his hands. The orb was now gone, although he had the other in his pocket, but it would not be needed. The man smiled to him and took five ten-pieces from his pocket, handing them to Chris with a pat on the back and a handshake. When their business wrap-up was finished, he headed back on his way to the tavern to meet up with the rest of the group.

Entering the tavern, he found the girls sitting at the table drinking their water. With a smile, he strolled over to the bar and obtained a glass from the tender, walking back over to the table and taking a seat. "So, what have my two favorite gals been up to today?"

Caitlyn smiled, filling his glass and saying, "We did a bit of trading. Darla made over a hundred gold on one of those pendants we brought from home." She pulled out the pouch and tossed it to Chris with a smile. "We also bought a cloak for me and Donnie so we won't look so suspicious.

"Awesome, Darla! Way to go, you two." He took the pouch, removing the coins from his own pocket and placing them within. "I, myself, made fifty on the roof job. I also got a repair orb along with it." He pulled it from his pocket and waved it before them, returning it. "Never know when this might come in handy. Speaking of which, I have some bad news. The spells in the tome have been erased." He went on to explain why, and the three discussed what could be done to make up for it.

The three continued to talk for a few minutes when a puzzled Donnie walked in. He walked over to the table and handed the letter to Chris. "Somebody knows that we're here."

Chris took the letter and examined the writing and the seal. "Where did you get this?"

"The clerk at the post office got this in a delivery that came today."

Caitlyn looked at it, saying, "Who would send us a letter?"

Chris shrugged and opened the seal, unfolding the letter. "We're about to find out." He looked it over briefly and began to read aloud:

"If you are reading this letter, then our prayers have been answered and the guardian spirits have come through for us. Something wicked is transpiring in the Forest of Night and the king has become terminally ill. Terrible things are happening in the capital province! You must hurry!"

"How very strange. Well, whatever the matter is, we have to help them. We have to help their king," Darla said.

"But who exactly are we helping? And how are we to help? That letter sure doesn't give us much to go on," said Caitlyn.

Chris laid the letter on the table and reread it silently. "Well, here's what we do know. Supposedly there is something we can do to help the king. Also, something is happening in the 'Forest of Night.' Was that on your map Donnie?" Donnie shook his head, so Chris continued. "Well, we'll have to figure out where that is. The king would be in the capital. We'll have to make that our first destination. That wasn't on your map either?"

"No. The guy has other maps, though, so I'll check again tomorrow."

"All right. Let's see. There's no signature, and that's all there appears to be to the letter. So I guess that means that we're just going to have to get there somehow and figure out what to do when we get there."

The three nodded. Chris took out the pouch and set it on the table. "Altogether, we should have enough gold to get a bit of supplies. Caitlyn, how much food do we have left?"

"We've got enough to last us about three days, three meals a day."

"All right. We'll see how far it is to the next town. If it isn't too far, we won't buy any food here. Oh yes, that reminds me, there's a bakery in town. The guy I helped is the town baker. He's giving us all dinner as part of my payment." The three smiled at that. "We're also going to need some form of protection."

Darla looked to Caitlyn and said, "Wasn't there a blacksmith in town?"

Caitlyn nodded and Chris commented, "There is, but he may overcharge a bit. He was going to charge the baker an arm and a leg to fix the roof. Apparently, he can use the orbs as well."

Donnie smiled and said, "Well, I should be able to use a sword fairly well. I've practiced with fake stuff, and it may not be that different."

"All right, Donnie. You'll be our main source of protection until I can find some spell that will allow me to do some damage. Darla won't have any spells that do much damage, I don't think."

"Maybe the blacksmith has some spell that you or I could use," Darla said.

"Well, as for me, I'm getting hungry. Let's get some lunch," said Donnie.

After lunch, the group walked around the town, getting a feel for the place. Each person pointed out where they had been. After a while, they went back to the tavern to chat and make plans. A couple of hours passed and the sun began to set.

"Isn't it about time to head to the bakery?" Donnie asked, turning to Chris.

"Yes, we probably ought to go on. It's beginning to get dark." The group headed out the door and down the main road of the town.

They found the bakery without problem and entered, the scent of fresh baked bread sweeping around them, furthering their desire to eat. Chris walked over to the counter to talk to the baker's wife and the rest took a seat at one of the two tables in the shop. "Hello. My name is Chris and these are my friends. I fixed your roof today."

"Ah yes, my husband came in and told me about it. I'm Eleanor. I help him with the shop, though he's quite talented on his own. He should be in to see you shortly. He went to go buy some things in the market place."

"That's quite all right," Chris replied. He walked over to the table, took off his cloak and placed it on the other table, as he saw the others had done, and sat down as the woman came from behind the main counter.

"Can I get you something to drink? We've got water, some berry and fruit juices, and a bit of ale."

Donnie and Darla asked for water, Caitlyn ordered orange juice, and Chris got a glass of fizzleberry juice, unique to the Gammeron Plains.

"Are you folks new around here?"

Donnie chuckled, replying, "That's an understatement."

"What my friend means is that we're not from around here. We traveled a long way to get here," said Darla.

The door opened and in came the baker. He walked over to his wife and gave her a kiss on the cheek, then walked over to the table, shaking Chris's hand. "Good to see you again, my boy. I trust my wife has been taking good care of you?"

"Oh yes, sir. We've received great treatment."

"That's good to hear. Can we get you four something to eat then?"

The four nodded and he walked back behind the counter to the hearth where bread had been baking. He took a loaf about the length of a man's arm and brought it over to the table to start slicing it. "Ellie, fetch some cheeses and jams for 'em."

The woman walked to a shelf to one side and took down two jars of jam, pouring a bit of each onto a wooden plate before her, then sliced a bit of three different types of cheeses and placed the slices on the plate, setting the knife on it then carrying it over to the table. "Here you go, some of my homemade cheese and jam. That one," she said, pointing to a light colored cheese, "is your basic Gammeron cheese. This one in thin slices is a bit spicier. The dark one here is a sharp cheese." She motioned next to the jams, saying, "The red one is a bit of apple jam and the black one is forest berry jam. It's got a nice tang to it. Enjoy."

As Eleanor walked back to the counter, Richard finished his cutting and walked back to meet her. Caitlyn looked to them and said, "Since you nice folks are being kind enough to provide us with dinner, and there's much more here than we can eat," she said, shooting a glance at Donnie, "then why don't you join us?"

"Oh, we couldn't. Like I said, its part of the payment for fixing the roof," Richard replied.

"We wouldn't think of it. Please, join us and tell us a bit about this area. We don't know too much about where we are, so a local opinion would be of great help," Chris told them.

The man looked to his wife as she shrugged, so the two of the walked over and pulled up chairs from the other table, the four scooting their own chairs to make room.

"So, what did bring you to this region?" the man asked.

Chris turned to Darla and quietly discussed what exactly to tell them. A robed man entered the bakery and walked up to the counter. Eleanor went over to serve him. Chris nodded to Darla, looked to the others and, with a nod from them, began to tell them the whole story as they started to eat.

"...And so we're standing here today. So you could say we're very new here."

"You mean—you young folks are from a whole other world? That's rather hard to believe. But...it would make a bit of sense out of the four of you. I can tell that you two definitely don't match the rest of us," Eleanor commented as she sat back down, the man having left, motioning to Caitlyn and Donnie who were wearing Earth clothing. "But you, Wizard, you look fairly normal. And you, missy, can I ask you, is that an Agape robe?" she asked Darla.

"Why, yes, it is."

"Thought so. My great aunt was an Agape priestess. She passed away not too long ago. She did leave me her stuff though. Think you could get any use out of it?"

"I probably could, ma'am, thank you. The journey will be long and hard."

"All right. Swing by the house tomorrow and I'll see what I have."

"Well, now what are you planning to do while you're here?" asked Richard.

"We've done a bit of things around town to gain some money," Chris said, motioning to the man about his roof. "And today we got a letter from some people in the capital province about an illness affecting the king and some kind of trouble in the 'Forest of Night.' We figure that we should go there first to see what it's all about."

"The king, you say? Well, that's rather strange. I'm certain someone would have brought word if something had been amiss. Very odd," Eleanor commented.

"Well, if it's the capital you need to get to, you'll have to take the Blue Mountain Pass. It'll be about eight day's journey, by foot."

"Eight days? That's quite a long walk," said Caitlyn.

"It will be longer than that," Donnie said, arousing a puzzled look from the others. "The guy that brought the mail said there was a rockslide in the mountains. I would assume he was talking about on the pass."

"A slide on the pass? That's definitely not good. To find your way across those mountains without using the pass would take at least another three or four days," the baker said.

"Oh no! I don't think we'd even have enough money to buy the supplies for that," Darla said.

"Well, we'd love to help you, but our bread wouldn't last more than three or four days before getting stale," said Richard.

"Is there any other way to get around those mountains?" Chris asked.

"Well, there is one way," the man replied. "But it is very unlikely to happen. The supply boats in the dock occasionally take passengers, but they don't do it cheap. Not unless you're sent by the mayor, but getting to see him beyond tax day is next to impossible."

"When's the next tax day?" asked Donnie.

"Oh, in about a month," said Eleanor.

"Well, that won't do us much good. I guess we'll just have to go find out their price," said Chris with a sigh.

Chris was the first to notice how late it was, and made the suggestion that they retire for the night. The four of them said goodbye to Richard and Eleanor and walked back to the inn. Donnie and Caitlyn were already yawning by the time they entered the door, so they said goodnight and headed for the stairs.

"I'll be up in a bit, Donnie; I'm going to look over those maps you brought. Sleep sound," said Chris as he walked over to their table, taking from his pocket the two maps Donnie had copied and setting them on the table.

Darla had followed Caitlyn to the stairs, but turned back, spotting Donnie and Chris and overhearing what he said. She looked to Caitlyn and told her that she would stay down as well to get a drink of water before she went to bed. Caitlyn looked at her for a second, knowing that her intentions were not truthfully stated, but shrugged and walked up the stairs, Donnie following shortly behind.

Darla walked over to the table and pulled up a chair next to Chris, saying, "So, this is where we're at right now?"

"Yes. Here's Kelara Bay, here's the forest in which the mayor's house should be. This road appears to lead to the foot of the mountains." He paused slightly and continued. "According to the map, if it is drawn to scale, then the estimates made by Richard and Eleanor should be quite correct."

Darla noticed the slight waver in his voice and scooted her chair a bit closer, asking, "What's the matter, Chris?"

"It's—nothing. It's not important."

"Please, tell me."

"Well, I'm just not certain about much of anything right now." He sighed. "Do you think I'm a good leader?"

"Yes, of course I do. You've done a great job so far."

"Yeah, but—we've not even started the journey. It's going to get really hard once we get too deep in this. I'm just afraid—that I won't be the right person to lead you guys."

"What are you saying? You're the most powerful one of us here. You've got a lot of wisdom and maturity, and that makes you a good leader. You're very trustworthy and you've done nothing but look out for the well-being of the group."

He looked at her for a second and sighed again. "I guess you're right. I care about you guys a lot. I realize that I pulled you into a situation that not one of you asked to be in or even would want to be in."

"I know that it's hard. It's hard for all of us. But I think that we all realize our duty here. I personally have no clue why I was one of the four of us. I know that there is bound to be a reason, but I don't know it yet. I think we'll all find out what role we play here."

"Yeah. You're right. I just can't wait to see what the other two are to become. I bet they'll be fantastic." He smiled a bit. "We're a team. We've all got our part to play."

Darla nodded and smiled as well. She reached over and took his hand in hers softly. "Everything will work out. I'm sure."

As she held his hand, Chris felt a strange sense of connection to her. It was as if the magic they had inside them was almost shared, linking them together. A feeling of contentment washed over him as her fingers touched his.

He did not know, however, that she felt the same thing. As she looked into his eyes, a strange, yet comforting calm fell over her. It was the same feeling she had that night they spent in the hammock. They became lost in each other's eyes, forgetting the clatter and chatter in the tavern. Darla caught herself shortly, though, and let go of his hand. She muttered a bit hesitantly, "I'm going, um, to head up to bed now, I guess."

"See you then. Sleep sweetly," he said with a bit of a sigh.

Darla walked up the stairs and into her room, noticing that Caitlyn was already asleep. *She must really have been bushed from all that shopping*, she thought with a silent chuckle. She walked over to the window and leaned against the wall, looking out into the night sky and to the ocean visible just beyond the houses and buildings of the town. A slight chill hit her and she wrapped her cloak even tighter around her.

She began to examine herself and what she was going through. *Could it really be that there was something more there? Surely not,* she thought. *But—it was so wonderful to be with him. He makes me feel so peaceful, so calm. It's like we are two parts of the puzzle that were meant to be side by side.* She sighed, taking a deep breath. *I know it can't be, though. I have to focus on the tasks at hand. Besides, he doesn't feel the same way. He didn't feel anything for me before his change, and he doesn't now; I'm sure of it. There's nothing there, Darla. Just focus on what really matters.* She felt a tear come to her eye and brushed it off, walking over to the mattress-like bedroll, taking off her cloak, and lying down, wrapping a blanket around her snugly. She continued to think, but eventually found herself in the quiet peace of sleep.

* * *

75

Chris continued to look over the maps for a while, planning a bit here and there, noting some things of interest. Eventually he stopped and folded up the maps, placing them inside his pocket. He stood up and wrapped his robe around him, lifting the hood to cover his head as he stepped out into the night. He walked a few steps and heard the sound of a sigh, turning and looking to see no one. However, as he turned his eyes, he looked up slightly and caught the image of a woman in a window above. He recognized her as Darla and looked at her for a few seconds. The moonlight was catching off her skin in just such a perfect way that it seemed almost as if she was nothing more than a specter, a fantasy, to fade as the moon gave way to the sun. He gazed at her for just a short time before she turned away and walked back into her room.

He sighed deeply and walked down the main road for a while, spotting no one as he walked. He began to fight himself over what he had felt not an hour ago. "I'm being highly irrational," he said to himself. "It was nothing more than a simple friendly touch, one friend to another. She was trying to reassure me, nothing more.

"But she was so beautiful in the window. What am I saying? I can't be feeling this. These emotions aren't going to get anyone anywhere. I've got the group to think of now. I cannot let them down. Besides, I'm certain that there is no way she could feel anything of the same for me. Even with this change, I'm still the same old me I've always been."

He sighed once more and walked back to the inn to rest his body, though his mind would see no rest in sleep. Tomorrow was going to be a long day.

The group assembled in the tavern of the inn just a bit after sunrise. "Donnie, you go ahead and return to the post office and get the map on the capital's province. Darla, you and Caitlyn go to Eleanor and see what she has. I'll go to the docks and see what kind of prices they offer. Let's meet back in, say, hour and a half?" The three nodded and they all started out the door.

Donnie walked back toward the post office, passing some

townspeople as he went. They seemed a bit friendlier than before, now that he faintly resembled one of them. He had his cloak wrapped around him so that his Earth clothing couldn't be seen very well. He stepped into the post office and walked up to the counter, wishing the man a good morning.

"Hello there. I don't believe I've seen you around before, new in town?"

"Well, no. I was in here yesterday, looking at the maps? I was wearing—odd clothing at the time."

"Ah, yes. The traveler. Something I can do for you?"

"Yes, actually. Do you know your way around the capital province?"

"I sure do, son," the man smiled. "Lived there for a right long bit back in my younger days. I was a post boy for the castle, I was. Anything you need to know?"

Donnie nodded and smiled, saying, "Yes. I need to know a bit about the places around the capital."

"Well, let's see here. There's a little village right outside the castle town, by the name of Woodsmith Village. I had a friend who lived there once. My, he was a feisty one, he was. One time, he and I were at the castle docks, and there was this seagull, you see, so he—"

Donnie noticed that he was beginning to ramble so he spoke up. "Um, sir. You were talking about the city?"

"Oh, yes, sorry 'bout that. The city…yes…the city. It isn't too big of a place. It's mostly known for the woodcrafters there. Yep, they have some of the best woodsmiths there around, hence the name of the village." The man smiled, clearing out his throat a bit with a chuckle. "My buddy, he would always go get wood from the forests around and chop it up and bring it to the smithy. One time, he was out there chopping some wood and he saw this rabbit. Darned if it wasn't the biggest dang rabbit you ever woulda seen. Well, he up and started chasin' after it and 'round sundown—"

Donnie sighed and interrupted again. "Sir, uh, could you tell me about a particular forest?"

The man caught himself again with a chuckle, nodding his head. "Which one do you want to know of? There's the forest you come into right off the mountain, it's got some of the best trails for hiking you ever saw. Then there's a forest around back of the castle which has this lake they use to fill the castle moat."

"Well, I'm more interested in the 'Forest of Night' I heard of."

The man took a slight pause, arching his brow at the young man. "Why would you be wanting to know about that place?"

"Well, we heard there were something going on there that we wanted to go see and—"

"There isn't anybody there worth seeing, lest you want to get yourself in a lot of trouble, or worse than that, sleeping in a six-foot-deep hammock."

Donnie's eyes widened a bit. "Sir, we think there may be some people near there that need our help, my friends and I. Can you please tell me about it?"

The man sighed softly and, with a long pause, began to speak again. "My brother went into that forest and didn't come out. Not many family lines in Woodsmith Village can say they ain't ever lost someone to that forest. In the daytime, no matter what time of the year, the forest is barren and dull. But at night, it's like you're in a totally different forest. Things change. You can't tell from the outside and I never dared to go in, but I've heard stories. And the plants aren't the only things that change. The animals—something happens to them as well. If someone you know in is in that forest, the best thing to do is to let 'em stay there."

Donnie nodded slowly, saying, "Hmm. Well—anyways, can I get the map for the capital province?"

The man sighed and nodded, taking out the stack of maps and pulling out the map for the capital. Donnie walked down the counter with the paper and took out his own, starting to copy.

* * *

Darla and Caitlyn walked down the main road, looking for the house Chris had described to them. They eventually spotted it and walked up, knocking on the door. Eleanor opened it and smiled, waving them in. "Rich is at the bakery this morning. How are you girls doing?"

"We're pretty good, ma'am. How are you today?" Darla asked.

"Oh, doing pretty good, I say. It looks to be a pretty nice day today. I've been looking for the stuff I promised you. Found it in a chest in the spare bedroom."

She smiled and walked back through the house, coming back out with bag that resembled a backpack and a wooden staff with gold leaves and tendrils near the top. "Here you go."

"Thanks. Wow, this is a beautiful staff. Let's see what we got in here," said Darla. She walked over and leaned the staff against the wall, sat on a chair and opened the pack. She reached inside and pulled out a small book entitled *Herbal and Mineral Magicks*. "This should be useful. What else have we here?" She pulled out two long, white gloves. She looked them over, noticing that they were of a thin, silk-like cloth, with dark blue embroidery on the backs. "These are very pretty."

"Yes, her mother gave them to her just as she entered with the priestesses."

"Well, let's see how these look on me." She set them down and unclasped the bracelet Chris gave her and set it to the side. She pulled on one of the gloves, smiling as the soft fabric wrapped around her fingers. She pulled on the other one and wiggled her fingers. She reached into the pack again, noticing that it was much easier to maneuver with these gloves on than any others. She pulled out a small orb. As she examined it, she saw that was a clear orb that seemed to have a quill pen inscribed inside.

"What kind of spell is that, Darla?" Caitlyn asked.

Darla wrapped her hands around the orb, focusing her mind. "Oh my goodness, this is an inscription orb! It can create a spell in the tome that I'll be able to always use!"

"Awesome! Anything else in there?"

"Hmm. Let's see." She turned the pack over and as she shook it a bit, a piece of paper falling out. Darla began to read it aloud.

"To the receiver of my gifts: My niece has kindly given you some tools that you'll find very helpful to you in whatever you may do. All sisters carry a staff as it is given from High Priestess to Initiate. That is what I do now, even though it happens to be posthumously. It is the only major defense you are allowed to have.

"My Agape sister, the road is not kind. You must rely on your friends as they will rely on you. It is of the utmost important that you visit the high temple at least once during your life to gain the blessings of the Great Priestess. I believe that you will go far, my sister.

"Below, I have scribed the words of the spell to heal small wounds. I would greatly suggest that you inscribe it into your tome, if you have one. It will come in handy. With the love of the Goddess, Maria, High Priestess of Agape."

Written just below the signature was the healing spell she mentioned. Darla smiled and placed the letter in a pocket within her cloak. She took the orb and placed it there as well. "Eleanor, I must thank you for these gifts. They will be very helpful to us."

"Well, you ought to thank my aunt for them," she replied with a chuckle.

Caitlyn smiled, saying, "Thanks a lot for all your help, ma'am." She turned to Darla, saying, "We probably should be returning to the inn to wait for the others."

Darla nodded and stood, Caitlyn and Eleanor following suite. The girls said goodbye and headed out.

* * *

Chris walked down the road to the docks, a light breeze blowing his cloak around his legs. He arrived at the docks to see only a few boats on the water. Several men were walking back and forth, carrying boxes on and off the ships. Chris inquired to one of the men as to which ship would be traveling to the capital province soon and the man replied by silently pointing at one. Chris headed toward that one, noticing that it was a two-mast cargo boat, its sails down. Chris walked up the gangplank, noticing the words, *The Cutter*, on the side. He had to step over a bit as one of the shipmen came barreling down, having very little regard for the wizard, and onto the deck, looking around for someone that might seem in charge. He saw a large, gray-haired and gray-bearded man, dressed in slightly nicer clothing, talking to another man who looked to be about the same build, dressed in more work-oriented clothes. Chris walked up to him with a fairly confident step.

"Hello sir. Are you the captain of this ship?"

The man looked at Chris, arching a brow. "Yes, I am. Who are you and what are you doing on my ship?"

"I'm just a traveler. I've come to ask for passage to the capital."

The man looked at him for a second, turning to the other and whispering a bit. "Is it just you going?"

"No, sir, I've got three friends."

The man turned and conversed more, turning back with a slight smirk. "It's not easy taking passengers on a cargo ship. I've got barely enough room for the men, let alone a few stragglers. It'll cost you."

"How much?"

The man thought for a minute, placing his hand to his whiskery chin. "I can't afford to take you for any less than…three hundred gold, a piece."

Chris's eyes widened, saying, "Three hundred gold? Why, that's way too much!"

"I'm sorry kid, take it or leave it."

"Please, sir, we've got to get to the capital province as soon as we can. The king needs our help."

"The king?" the man said with a slight chuckle. "Look kid, I can't do any better than that price. Trade has been slow these past couple of months. I can't cut anyone any breaks, save those on official business from the mayor and if the king had needed you, he would have been told. This ship sets out tomorrow no more than an hour after sunset. Either you make my price or you find some other way. I warn you, though: there won't be another ship in from the capital for at least another week or two. After I hit there, I'm heading further up the coast."

Chris sighed and nodded turning and walking back down the plank.

7

A One-Way Ticket

The four eventually met back up in the tavern, Chris arriving first, then Donnie, and finally the girls. As they sat down, Darla let Donnie look at her staff while she and Chris discussed the new spell. "Should I go ahead and copy this healing spell into our book?"

Chris nodded, replying, "Most definitely. Until we get a higher caliber spell, this will probably be the most useful. Go ahead."

Darla took the slip of paper from her cloak as well as the orb and placed them on the table. She reached into the air to pull out the tome and set it on the table as well. Flipping to the first page, she took the inscription orb in hand and thought for a second. "How exactly do I go about this?"

Chris shrugged and said, "I'm not quite sure. Here, go ahead and focus on the orb and I'll place the spell on the page and we'll see what happens from there."

Darla nodded and clasped her hands around the orb, beginning to channel some energy into it. As it began to glow, Chris picked up the piece of paper and started to move it onto the book but stopped as suddenly the words began to glow. As Darla continued to focus, the words seemed to begin to flow off the page, a bright white wisp of power, connecting between the book and page, each letter seeming to be stripped off into the light. Caitlyn and Donnie turned to watch the scene unfold as well.

The wisp, like a long tendril of thread, began to move upon the page in the book, writing in each letter of the spell. After a few seconds, the tendril began to fade and Darla eventually opened her empty hands. The page was now blank, save the words of the message, and where a blank page had been in the tome now laid a full page, the words of the spell scribed upon it.

"Well, that was quite interesting. Care to try the spell out, Darla?" Caitlyn asked.

"How precisely am I going to do that?"

"Well, let's see. Hey, Chris, come here."

Chris backed up a bit, shaking his head. "Oh no, you're not doing anything to me."

"Well, then, how about you, Donnie?"

Donnie sighed and said, "All right, all right. I'll be your guinea pig."

Caitlyn nodded and picked up a knife from the table. "Here, give yourself a small cut."

Donnie took the knife and grimaced a bit, placing his hand down on the table. "You will heal me, right?"

Darla replied, "I'll do my best."

Donnie took the tip of the knife and sliced into his palm about an inch across, blood quickly beginning to flow from the cut. "Okay, ouch, please fix this."

Darla nodded and took his hand in hers, placing her other palm over the cut and beginning to chant the incantation, finding it surprisingly fresh in her memory even without looking at the page. A faint white glow emerged from between their hands and in just a few seconds, it was gone. Darla raised her hand to show her palms clean and his hand clean and uncut. Donnie examined his hand with a smile. "Nice work."

Darla smiled and turned to Chris, saying, "Well, we'll just have to see how minor a cut has to be to get caught in my spell. She turned to pick up the book and noticed that the page was blank again. "Chris, look!"

He looked at the page and arched a brow. "I thought the spell was supposed to stay!"

Darla flipped through a few pages then eventually came back to it. "I don't understand what could have gone wrong. It's supposed to—" She stopped when she noticed that some words began to appear on the page, a very faint gray. After a couple of seconds another word appeared. "Wait, I think I understand. It's coming back, very slowly. I think I have to wait a while between castings. Come to think of it, I can't remember the words to the spell now, either. I could just a second ago, though."

Chris nodded, saying, "I bet my spells will be the same way. We'll have to find out just when the spell recharges. I did find out how much they want for passage."

"How much?" asked Donnie.

"Well, the captain said he won't take us for less than three hundred gold—"

"Hey, we've got nearly that much. Surely we can raise the rest," said Caitlyn.

"—A piece."

"What?" Darla exclaimed. "There's no way!"

"Unfortunately, that's his price. Unless we're on official business from the mayor, we won't get anywhere anytime soon. And he's leaving out tomorrow."

The other three sighed. Donnie spoke up, saying, "Well, how about we go talk to the mayor? His house is about a two-hour walk outside of town. Maybe he'll help us."

"Highly doubtable," Darla said with another sigh. "But what other choice do we have?"

Chris nodded, saying, "All right. After lunch we'll start for the mayor's."

"Hey Chris?" Donnie asked. "We ought to stop by the marketplace before we go. I want to check out the blacksmith shop and see what we can get. We'll need some sort of protective weapon."

"I agree," Chris said. "It'll definitely be necessary if we run into some trouble. I don't know what to expect from this mayor."

* * *

The four ate a rather filling lunch in the tavern, finding that the keeper had some boar roasting over the fire. Darla had gone down to the bakery and picked up half a loaf of fresh bread, the baker kindly giving it for free. After their meal, they all walked down to the marketplace, each person cloaked, with Darla holding her staff in gloved hands. The sun was about to hit the center of the sky and Donnie, remembering that he had a watch on, discovered that the time progressed in pretty much the same format as on Earth, his watch showing him that it was around 11:00 A.M. in the other world. They walked around for a bit, glancing at the various merchants.

Located in the back of the marketplace, at least from where they entered, they came to the smithy. The blacksmith stood over a hot fire, getting a piece of metal ready to become one thing or another. He was a rugged man of a bit taller than average stance, very strong in appearance, with a sheen of sweat covering his brow, back, and chest where it could be seen behind his work apron. He walked over to his anvil and placed the piece down, striking it a couple of times with his hammer, before dipping it in some water to cool it off.

The girls stood a bit behind as Donnie and Chris walked up to the man. He stood up straight, wiping a bit of the sweat from his brow. "What can I get for you, gents?"

Chris glanced around a second, noticing several swords, staves, pieces of armor, etc. "Well, we need some kind of weapon. We're about to start out on a journey and I think it would be a wise choice to equip ourselves with more than just this staff here." He motioned to Darla.

"Ah! Which one of you is going to need a weapon?"

"Well, my friend here, and something for myself, if possible," Chris replied.

The man nodded and walked over to a rack of swords. Donnie and Chris followed him, glancing at the various blades, each one appearing to be finely crafted, some with very simple design, still others with rather ornate carvings and hilts. "I can tell that you're a sword man, correct?"

"Yes, sir. I do take to them," Donnie replied.

"Well, here are my blades. The shorter ones are around eighty gold, the larger ones around one-fifty. Take your pick."

Donnie eyed them over; taking down a short sword that had a strange, flame pattern down the blade with a hilt that had a ruby on each side and small jets of flame carved upon it. He lifted it and swung it a bit to get a feel for the weight. "How much for this one, sir?"

"Ah! That's a fine blade there. Strong, strong metal. I might let it go for, say, one-twenty?"

Donnie turned to Chris and the two quietly discussed the transaction. He turned back to the man and said, "I don't know. You see, the rubies are quite nice and all, but the hilt is a little weighty. It might give me a bit of trouble. How about—one hundred?"

"Now, now. I quite fancy that hilt. I don't think a hundred would do it justice. How about a hundred and ten?"

"Hmm. I guess we might be able to part with that much," Donnie said with a smile. Chris took the pouch from within his robe, counting out the payment and giving it to the man.

The smithy took the gold with a smile, saying, "Thank you. I'm sure it'll do you proud. If you ever have any problems with it, bring it back here and I'll fix 'er up, no charge."

"Thank you, sir," Donnie said.

"Oh and here. You'll be needing a sheath for it. I've got a belt and frog that'll be just right for you." The man turned to a small box and pulled out a black, leather belt and a another piece that had two loops above it to go on the belt and a little sleeve below, not more than four or five inches long, to hold the sword. Donnie took it and turned around, sliding the belt through the loops in his jeans, adding the frog along with it. Once he had it on, he slid the sword in the sleeve and practiced drawing it out and replacing it.

As he was doing this, Chris walked over to the staves that were leaning against one wall. He picked up one made of a very firm looking wood and hefted it, feeling out the balance. He placed it down and picked up another one. He looked it over, noticing the carvings up and down the wood. He noticed at the top that there were

three small, carved figures, runes of sorts. "Tell me about this staff."
"That's a fine staff, there. A wizard sold that to me as he was passing through a couple of years ago. It's got an enchantment on it. He was passing through the Northern provinces and needed a way to fight off some of the cold creatures up there, so he enchanted his staff to be able to shoot fire from the tip."
"So you mean this staff will shoot fire?"
"Well, not anymore. It was quite a long time ago and the enchantment has faded with time. The effect has been reduced a bit. It can start little fires, like campfires and whatnot, but nothing major. I suppose if you got close enough to something, you could do a small bit of damage, but not much."
"I see. How much for it?"
"Well, being that it's enchanted and all, I suppose I could let you have it for—say, ninety gold?"
"Ninety? That is a little steep. After all, that sword did take a bite out of our reservoir. I don't know if I could go more than…fifty?"
The man looked rather offended, saying, "Fifty? For that fine piece of work? Why, I couldn't buy it off that wizard for less than seventy!"
"Okay, seventy, then."
"Well—all right. But I'm losing money here."
Chris smiled and took the gold from the pouch, handing it to him. "Thank you very much. It was nice doing business with you." The two guys turned and walked away from the smithy, not seeing either of the girls. They looked around a bit and spotted the girls at one of the carts, glancing over some merchandise. The girls noticed their approach and turned to greet them. Donnie took out his sword and Chris hefted his staff, telling them of the special ability. The girls gave their "oohs" and "ahs" and looked over the weapons.
Darla smiled, saying, "These will definitely help a lot."
Caitlyn smiled as well, but her smile darkened a bit as she said, "They will, but…what about me?"
Chris replied, "I'm sorry, Caitlyn. I totally forgot. We're going to need the money we have left to buy supplies, should we be able to get

through to the mayor and get him to get us over there."

Caitlyn sighed and nodded as the four began to walk back to the tavern. "I understand. It may be best for me to just stay here while you guys go. I can wrap up things with the innkeeper and hang out in the tavern to listen to the passersby and see if there is anything else I can learn."

"Yeah, Catie, that would be rather helpful. It is probably a better idea for you to stay here until we can get you something to defend yourself with," Darla said.

The four approached the tavern as Chris said, "If you can, stay inside the tavern and near the innkeeper until we get back. We shouldn't be any later than about sundown getting back, I hope. It depends on how long it takes us with the mayor. I don't want anything happening to you, all right?" Chris said as he walked over and gave her a light hug.

"All right. You guys be careful, okay?"

"We will," replied Darla, giving her a hug as well.

"Don't get into any trouble," Donnie said with a chuckle.

The three started down the road as Donnie took the set of maps from his pocket, pulling out the one for their journey. "There is a road that leads to his house. Let's turn here."

After about an hour's walk or so, they could no longer see the village as they had first climbed the hill they had started out on and were now on the other side of it. They stopped to take a rest, sitting down on the bank of another hill. "Think Catie's gonna be all right, Darla?" asked Donnie.

"Yeah, she's a smart girl," she replied.

"I hope this mayor guy is worth our trouble. The lady in the town hall didn't have such a high regard for him."

They continued along the path, walking through a green meadow, wildflowers in blossom along each side of the trail and down through the fields. The sun was warm, but there was a light breeze blowing, reassuring them that it was autumn, but still early enough in the season to not be very cold. They could see the forest just ahead of them and knew that their destination was approaching swiftly.

As they entered the forest about an hour or so further into their walk, the trail became a bit harder to follow, and they realized that they were slowly rising up another hill. The trees spread out in each direction, large, leafy, and beautiful, with their roots spread along the ground, sometimes giving them a better foothold, sometimes causing a bit of deterrence to their path. Eventually they reached a bit of a clearing where stood a large, log house, built with ornate design, trimmed in gold and silver, with lavish landscaping, showing that it was paid for at no small expense.

The three walked up to the door, Chris stepping forward to knock on it lightly. After a few seconds had passed, he knocked again. Shortly after, it partially opened and a small man, a little less than Chris's height, stepped out. He had a rather smug look on his face and said, rather gruffly, "What do you want?"

"We've come to see the mayor," said Chris.

"No one gets in to see the mayor," the man replied and began to shut the door.

Donnie unsheathed his sword and placed his hand on the door, stopping it's close. "I don't believe you heard my friend. We want to see the mayor."

"Oh, really," he said, not shaken at all. He snapped his fingers and, stepping behind him, came a rather tall, rather well built man, carrying a much larger sword. "I don't believe you heard me, either. I said no one gets in to see the mayor."

Donnie stepped back, sheathing his sword rather quickly. The two men stepped fully out and pulled the door to, the larger one saying, "Are these people causing trouble?"

"No, Bruno, they're not causing any ruckus. They were just leaving. Isn't that right?"

Chris turned to look at the others then turned back to the two at the door. "Look, we don't want any trouble. We just need to speak to the mayor."

"If you need to speak to me, you must learn to ask nicely." The

90

door opened fully, revealing a tall, slim man, dressed rather nicely. "Politeness goes a long way." The two stepped aside as the man came out. "I am Mayor Brickshire. Come into my study." The mayor turned and walked back into the house, Chris, Donnie, and Darla following behind him. The small man and Bruno exchanged rather displeased looks and followed behind them, shutting the door.

"You'll have to excuse Bruno and Paradamus. They're a lot of help, being my main bodyguards, but they're also a lot of trouble," said the mayor. He walked down one hall to a room in the back, opening a door and shutting it behind the four of them. "Now, what can I do for you?" he asked as he walked behind his desk.

"Sir, we'd like to get passage to the capital province," Chris stated.

"Hmm. Passage to the capital, you say. Why exactly do you need to go there?"

"Well, you see, we received a letter requesting our help. We think that the king needs our help. It has something to do with the Forest of Night."

The man's eyes brightened up a bit. "The king, you say? Do you have that letter with you?"

"Yes, sir," said Donnie as he took the letter from within his cloak. He placed it on the desk. Brickshire took it and read through it, folding it up and examining the seal. "This is the royal seal, all right. You got this letter from the castle, did you?"

"We did? It wasn't signed, so we didn't—"

The mayor interrupted Chris mid-sentence, saying, "Well, regardless, if the king is in trouble, you need to get over there." He took a piece of paper from his desk and a quill pen, jotting out a letter. He folded it, took a bit of wax from a nearby candle, and sealed it, pressing in with a ring he wore. He flicked off a bit of wax from the ring and handed the letter to Chris.

Chris took notice of the imprint, a flourished set of initials: MEB. "Thank you, sir."

"Show that to the captain of *The Cutter*. It should be the one going to the capital. He and I are friends. Realize, now, that the only reason

I'm doing this for you is because the king needs you. Without him in power, I wouldn't stay in power, and I wouldn't make the tidy sum I make in this town." He chuckled a bit at that. "Frankly, you wouldn't have even gotten in to see me had I not taken an interest in your little group."

"Excuse me?" Darla asked.

"I was in town, disguised, when you were in the bakery. I remember another person in your group. Is she back in town?"

"Yes, sir. Wait, you were the man in the robes, weren't you?" Donnie asked.

He nodded and continued. "Yes. I overheard your story and found it quite interesting. I recognized the three of you as you were approaching. I was upstairs and saw you through a window. You know, I wouldn't recommend you telling that story to just anyone you meet. It's very naive and rather dumb. If people know you're new around, they won't hold back in trying to scam you. Trust me; I do it all the time."

Darla smirked, remembering the trader in the marketplace. "Well, thank you for your help. We ought to get going, right, Chris?"

Chris nodded, saying, "Yeah. We had better go. Thank you very much for your help, sir."

"You're welcome. And don't be telling any of my townspeople that I'm doing you a favor. They all think I'm a heartless beast, and I'd like to keep it that way."

"Why?" asked Darla.

"Because I am, of course," he answered with a rather unsettling laugh.

The three walked away from the house and back down through the forest, discussing the mayor and their plans for the journey. "He's rather odd. One second he's nice, the next he's mean. Very strange," remarked Darla.

"Eh, he's a politician," said Donnie with a chuckle.

They came to the edge of the forest, noticing that the sun was getting lower in the sky. "We should get back by sundown, as planned," said Chris as they began to walk out.

Suddenly, a gruff voice came up from behind them. "I want your gold and I want it now." Darla screamed, dropping her staff, as the tall, strong looking man grabbed onto her arm and slung her against his chest, wrapping an arm around her neck, holding a dagger in the other hand to her neck. Donnie and Chris swung around to face the man.

"It's you, the jackass from the other day," shouted Donnie with an apprehensive, but still confident attitude.

"Ah, I remember you now. You're the maid with the nice rear, aren't ya?" the man said, looking down at Darla.

"Look, we don't want any trouble," Chris stated, taking the gold pouch. "Let her go and you can take the money."

"Toss it here, boy. Do it quick, now, so that this pretty young wench doesn't get hurt." He tossed the pouch towards the man, his dagger hand catching it. Darla flinched as the dagger moved closer to her. "That's good, that's good. How much in here?"

"About thirty, forty gold. Let her go now, you've got your coins," Donnie stated, feeling anger rise in his chest.

"That all? Now, that weren't worth my trouble. Maybe I should take this lass here as the rest of my plunder."

A look of terror came over Darla's face as she realized his intent. Her eyes pleaded with Donnie and Chris for help.

"No, let her go. You can have our stuff, too, just let her go," Chris shouted.

"No, Chris, he's going to let her go. Light your staff," Donnie ordered, a confident tone in his voice.

"Now, I wouldn't try anything funny, kid, or this dagger will find a new home."

Chris looked at Donnie, a light flame encasing the top of the staff. "Donnie, what—"

Before he realized what was happening, Chris saw Donnie scream at the top of his lungs, unsheathing his sword and jumping in the air, flipping over the man's shoulder. As he landed, the startled man turned to face him, his side meeting Donnie's blade.

With a cry of pain, he dropped the dagger and pouch and clutched his side. Darla pulled away and ran to Chris's side, burying her face against his chest as he wrapped his arms around her. Donnie pulled his blade from the man's now bleeding side and stood silently. The man looked at him for just one moment before staggering off a few feet, dropping to the ground before he could get too far away.

A strong wind blew through the air, wrapping around Donnie as his very soul was filled with the images and voices that had penetrated the other two. He grasped his head but was able to maintain his composure. The eyes, however, caused him to shake slightly. Donnie bent down and picked up the dagger and pouch, standing back up. As he rose, he appeared taller, stronger. His hair was still short, but was no longer curly, but framed his head in a smooth, powerful stance. His body seemed to grow in muscle tone, but it appeared sleek and agile. He still wore his cloak, but beneath was a twill, brown tunic and black, leather pants. At his legs were leather boots that strapped at the shins. His sword still dripped blood as he slid it back into the frog.

Darla looked at him, seeming shocked for a few seconds then smiling. Chris and Darla walked over to him, Chris grinning and extending his hand to him, the two men grasping each other's wrists and pulling into a brother's embrace. "It's good to have you aboard now, warrior!"

"I feel…very strong, very brave. I'm a warrior now?"

Chris nodded with a smile. "You're our warrior. Three down, one to go."

Darla gave him a hug as well, thanking him for saving her life. The three walked over to the man, now dead. They uncovered his face, seeing it scarred and brutal. Chris searched the man, finding two pouches of gold and another dagger. "He won't be needing these now, I'd suspect."

"I—I killed a man? My hands, my sword. I killed—" The adrenaline now wearing off, the severity of the situation came to him.

"Donnie, he was going to take Darla. It was your appointed time anyways. I believe that in this world, we can't just fall prey to whoever wishes to hurt us. This is a different time and place now. You did what was right, saving Darla. If I could have, I would have laid my life down to save her, as I'm sure you would as well."

Darla smiled, walking over to pick up her staff and returning to Chris's side. They left the man there as they returned to the path, heading for the bay. Donnie placed the second dagger in his cloak with the first one. He tossed their original pouch to Chris.

He opened one of the thief's, looking inside. "Why, there must be three or four hundred gold in here," he exclaimed, looking in the second one to find a similar amount.

The three of them approached the town, heading for the inn. As they reached the entrance, Caitlyn turned from her seat at the bar and saw them, hopping down and walking over to greet them. She noticed Donnie, with a smile, and congratulated him on his change.

"Thanks, Catie. This should make things a bit easier on us."

"So, did we get passage?"

"Yep," Chris replied, pulling out the letter. "We also had a run in with a would-be thief and kidnapper."

"Oh goodness! What happened?"

Donnie led the three over to their table and took a seat, the others following. "Well, it was how I changed. This guy came out of nowhere and grabbed Darla, saying 'Give me your gold!'"

Darla nodded, adding, "Yeah, he pulled a dagger on me and was threatening to kill me. Then, when he wasn't satisfied with just our gold, he threatened to take me away as well."

"What did you do?" Caitlyn asked.

"Well, Donnie looked at me," Chris continued, "and told me to light my staff. I did and before I knew it, he flipped over the guy's head and when he turned around, Donnie stabbed him."

"Yeah, I felt horrible afterwards, but we realized that it was either him or Darla, and it certainly wasn't going to be Darla."

Caitlyn smiled and nodded. "Go on!"

"Well, that's about all there was to it. We got our gold back," Chris said with a smile. "And speaking of, we searched his body and came up with two daggers and two bags of gold." He pulled the bags from his pockets, opening them up and taking the gold out onto the table. The four counted it out, finding that the sum was seven hundred twenty gold.

"I do believe we can get some more supplies with this, definitely. We'd better wait, though, until we get to the capital. We'll probably find some better stuff over there," Donnie said.

All of a sudden, Darla's eyes lit up. "I just remembered the spell. What was that, about seven or eight hours?"

"Yeah, good. That's not too long. Well, I'm going to go down to the dock and get things ready for the journey. Caitlyn, did you get things wrapped up with the innkeeper?"

"Yeah, we've got two more nights here, if we need them."

"All right. I'll be back shortly. Donnie, take those two daggers and teach Caitlyn how to use them. She can wield those until we get her something better." He started out the door into the dusk red evening as Donnie took the daggers from his cloak, handing them to Caitlyn.

8

Long Journey

By the next afternoon, the group was packed and ready to go. They stopped by the bakery to wish Richard and Eleanor farewell, eating lunch while they were there, and then headed to the dock. The sun was already beginning to head towards the horizon as they stepped up on the deck of *The Cutter*. The captain told them that they would reach the capital a couple of hours after dawn and that they would have to find a place on deck to sleep, as there wouldn't be anymore room below.

The four found a place at one rail that seemed less traveled and placed their packs there, generally keeping out of everyone's way. The hustle and bustle of the crew ensured that they would be run over if they didn't. By the time night had fallen, the ship pulled up anchor and set out from the dock, putting a few hundred feet between the shore and itself before turning and heading up the coast. In no time at all, they were approaching the mountains. It became obvious that there would have been no way to go around them as they formed steep cliffs at the rocky water's edge. Chris lit his staff to keep everyone warm as they talked. The night air wasn't really all that cool tonight; there just seemed to be a chill over the water. The gentle rocking on the calm water set them all at ease as the movement around the ship began to settle as well. The four of them sat around talking and made their way to sleep. The deck wasn't exactly comfortable so they used some of the extra clothes they had brought to form light pallets to sleep on, wrapping up in their cloaks.

As they settled to sleep, Darla couldn't seem to get her mind to stop thinking. The events of the day certainly brought into her mind a realization of the danger they were in. *But the boys were so brave today*, she thought. *Donnie was certainly valiant in his rescue. And Chris, willing to lay down all we had for my sake. "If I could have, I would have laid my life down to save her..."*

She continued to think as a memory came to mind.

As the tardy bell rang, Chris pulled a piece of paper from his backpack. He also took out a pen, beginning to write:

"Hi Darla. How are you? I'm going well. Time for another boring Algebra class. I swear, I've not enjoyed this class even one day this whole semester. It's ridiculous. So, what did you do this weekend? I went to the mall with Donnie. We saw a movie and hung out in the arcade for a bit. Other than that, no interesting news to report. I wish the weekend hadn't passed so quickly. Mondays are so boring. Did you do anything interesting?

"Write back. Chris."

He folded the note a few times, wrote "To Darla, from Chris" on the front, and passed the note to a friend in the next row and motioned to Darla. He handed her the note and she read the front with a smile and sent a glance his way. As the teacher began to go over the homework he'd assigned the Friday before, she opened up the note and began to read. Sitting near the back of the class made it easy to do things like passing notes without being caught.

She read over the note, pulling a pen from her pocket and jotting down her reply. She refolded the note and passed it back to Chris. He opened it and began to read:

"Hey Chris. Sounds like you had fun this weekend. I didn't do too much myself. I went shopping for some new jeans, but that was about it. I had a rather bad Sunday afternoon, though. I'll tell you about it later. Did you get the homework done? I had a bit of trouble with it. If you could stay after school today, we could go over it? Mom doesn't get off work until 4, so I'll be here until probably half past or so.

"Thanks, Darla."

With a smile, he wrote, "Of course. Meet me in the courtyard after the last bell." He passed it back to her and she read, looking to him with a nod.

At 3:30, the last bell rang and the halls were filled with the noise of students slamming locker doors, groaning over homework, and the sounds of the cars pulling out of the parking lot as every teen raced to free themselves from the campus. However, Darla was not walking to her car. Instead, she walked toward the picnic tables in the courtyard. Taking a seat at one, she pulled out her math book and flipped it open to the page they'd most recently worked on in class. Suddenly, she felt a hand on her shoulder and she jumped, turning around to see Chris standing behind her. With a chuckle and a gasp, she swatted at his hand playfully, saying, "Don't sneak up on me like that!"

He laughed and said, "Like what? Like some raving lunatic bent on your destruction?" He uttered a maniacal laugh and took a seat across from him, removing his book from his backpack and setting it on the table as well. "Ready to get started?" he asked with a smile.

"Sure. Let's see…. Yes, page 213. Here's what I'm having problems with. When you take the coefficient of this variable…"

After a bit of time, they were finished with the work and Darla felt fairly confident in her refreshed Algebra skills. At least, she felt confident enough not to bomb that part on the test. "Man, that went by pretty fast. I've still got at least another half hour to wait. You have someplace you need to be?"

"Not really. I'll stay with you until your mom gets here. It wouldn't be fair of me to leave you all alone, now would it?"

"Of course not. Heaven forbid it."

"So, any new developments on your front?"

She sighed a bit, saying, "Yeah. I told you how I had a bad weekend, right?"

"Yeah. What happened?"

"Well, my jerk boyfriend dumped me. He dumped me for that freshman cheerleader. I can't even remember her name. It's not important."

"Well, I sure am sorry to hear that. I won't say it, though."

"Won't say what? I told you so? Well, you did."

With a sigh, he nodded. "It was the same way with that other guy you dated. I just absolutely do not understand why girls date these complete jerks. I mean, it's almost like they don't even pay any attention to the really great guys out there," he continued, his voice seeming to pick up pace and intensity as he went along. "I mean, every day, some girl tells me that her boyfriend is a complete jerk. 'He's not romantic enough! He doesn't treat me like I want to be treated!' It's always the same things. My boyfriend did this, my boyfriend did that, blah, blah, blah!"

Darla looked at him with a rather blank expression on her face, signaling plainly to him that he was rambling again. When he snapped out of it, she replied, "Well, what do you expect? There are just no great guys out there anymore. I mean, you're like one of the only true male friends I have. You're smart, funny, and nice to hang out with, and you're really caring and compassionate."

"Oh please! No girl ever noticed anything about me that has made them want me as a boyfriend and, as far as this school goes, I highly doubt any ever will."

She sighed again with a nod, saying, "Well, unfortunately, I have to agree. Not to insult you, but more so to say that the majority of girls in our school are just plain shallow. Sooner or later someone will see how great you are. Just you don't worry."

"Yeah, yeah, it's the waiting part that kills me, though. Seems all I do is wait."

A chilled breeze blew onto the deck as Darla turned to look at him as he slept. She began to think about their past together, how they used to play on the elementary school playground together, how they seemed to always get put in the same classes during middle school. She remembered how he always seemed to be there to talk to her whenever one thing or another happened. Her memories were not of suffering through those hard times, however, but of time well enjoyed in his company. As he rolled over onto his side, she looked at him and smiled.

The sun rose brightly over the rail of the ship. Donnie was the first to wake up, stretching out a bit before standing up. He looked out to see where they were and saw a large, tree-spotted plain with some shapes on the horizon. The mountains could be seen in the distance behind them but ahead, nothing more than the coastline and the plains. Chris was next to wake up, standing and stretching beside Donnie. The guys let the girls sleep a little longer, knowing that it hadn't been the most restful of nights and that any extra sleep they could get would be greatly needed. The guys walked along the deck, noticing that not too many of the crewmembers had awakened yet. However, a few were up and around on deck, doing their duties.

As the girls woke up, not more than a half an hour later, a shape began to appear on the horizon. One of the crew members shouted to the captain, "The city is dead ahead, sir, and we've got clear sailing." The captain nodded back to the man and they both went back to their business.

The four travelers began to assemble their items, getting ready to disembark. As Chris went to get some information from the captain about stores and whatnot in the city, Donnie began talking to a few of the crewmembers to get similar info. The two returned to the girls to report on what they learned.

"There are a few good places to eat in the northern part of the city," said Donnie. "We'll land in the southwest part, but the city can be traversed rather easily by foot. I also got word of some of the better shops. It seems there are some places which will short change you at the drop of a hat, or should I say, a coin."

"Yeah, the captain said the same thing. He told me where the castle was and the best way to go about getting there," said Chris. "Well, before we land, I want to discuss something with you guys. We need to decide some things."

"What things, Chris?" asked Caitlyn.

"Well, first off, we need to choose a leader. Things could get ugly if there is trouble here and all four of us could very easily get into arguments with one another if we don't have one person in charge. What do you guys think?"

"I agree. Someone needs to be in charge," Caitlyn replied. "I don't feel like I could do it, so rule me out."

"Neither do I," remarked Darla. "I'm not very good with quick thinking."

"Well, Chris, you're really good with thinking. You're definitely the smartest of the four of us, and your magic is very powerful," Donnie said, patting him on the back.

"Yeah, but the wizard is never the leader. You're the strongest of us four. You'll be the most useful in a battle, as you can just rush in there and fight. I don't think I'll be able to wield a sword as well and I have to keep back and chant, anyways," Chris replied.

"Well, here's how I see it. Chris, you will be best at planning and directing us, so I think you should be the major leader of the group in the political, administrative sense," Darla said. "Donnie, however, you're going to be the best at handling any fighting or skirmish like that. You should be the guy that leads us in to battle."

"Sounds good to me," said Caitlyn.

Donnie turned to Chris and shrugged, saying, "I don't mind that plan. You?"

"Well, only if you three think I can handle it. I'm likely to make mistakes, being only semi-human," he said with a chuckle.

"I think you'll make a great leader," Darla said with a bright smile on her face.

"The other thing we need to discuss," Chris continued, "is what we go by. Seeing as how we're in a brand new place, with brand new bodies, at least, most of us, I think we should have new names. I mean, after all, Donnie Johnson doesn't exactly sound like a knight's name to me."

"Yeah," Donnie said with a nod.

"I've been tossing that idea around in my head and I think new names may be a way to establish our new identities in this world."

"Well, what, then, should the new names be?" Darla asked.

"Hmm. I used to go by the name 'Callidus Lanstone' in my gaming days. That could be my new name," said Chris.

"Yes, I remember you telling me about that, Chris. I like that name. Where did you get it from?" asked Caitlyn as she raised her mug, taking a drink.

"An old friend of mine, Josh, came up with it before my first role-playing game session."

"Ah, I remember him," Caitlyn said, suddenly remembering something else. "Hey, remember when my college test scores came back last year and they misspelled my name? It was Kailynn," she said, spelling it out. "I like that name. We'll say, Kailynn Belle."

"That definitely was a misspelling, but a cool name anyways. I like it," said Darla.

"All right, that leaves just me and Donnie," Darla said.

"Eh, I'm not partial. You guys pick a name for me," replied Donnie.

"Hmm. Well, Callidus and Kailynn are pretty close to Chris and Caitlyn. How could we change your name to suit your persona?" asked Darla as she thought.

Chris spoke up, saying, "Hey, we used to use 'Donnic' as your name in role-playing games? It's just one letter, but it'll work. How does that sound, eh?"

"Works for me," replied Donnie. "Let's say, Donnic Turnblade."

"Ah, a reflection of your style," Darla said with a chuckle. "Me next, me next."

"Well, you know, I like the name Darla in and of itself. It's got a kind of innocent charm to it," said Chris with a smile. Donnie and Caitlyn exchanged interested glances.

"Okay, I like my name as well. What about...Darla, Priestess of Agape? Simple, but it works," she said with a chuckle and a slight blush.

* * *

Chris smiled and, with a nod, said, "All righty. From here on out we are: Callidus, Donnic, Kailynn, and Darla. Try not to use the Earth names outside of private company."

Within the hour, the capital city became quite visible. It was apparently built on top of a hill, the port connected by a small road. There was a high wall around the main city that must have been taller than any of the buildings within the lower city as none could be seen above it besides the castle's main fortification. An opening in the wall could be seen where the dock road came out. There were two towers on each side of the entrance, most likely guard towers. The castle was the only thing visible beyond the wall. It was tall and grand, looking majestic against the horizon. It had several stone spires and towers jutting out from the main structure on each side.

"We'll reach the port shortly," said the captain as he walked over.

"Good, good. Thank you again for letting us travel with you. This certainly made our trip a lot easier," said Callidus.

"Well, the mayor said they needed you here, so I figured it would be best to just not argue. Besides, if the king needs you, you must be important." The captain returned to his duties and the group continued to talk as the ship came closer and closer to the city.

In no time, the ship arrived at the docks of the capital, several men awaiting it on the planks of the dock. The ship stopped, put in anchor, and the gangplank was dropped, several of the men heading onto the deck to unload the cargo. The group made their way down and out of the way, walking to the gate of the city. As they stepped inside the gate, the city became fully visible to them, an expansive lot of buildings, wooden, straw, very few stone buildings. The city was evenly built on the incline, the buildings rising slowly toward the castle, seen in the distance.

As they walked down the path from the docks, the sounds of the bustling city surrounded them. They found themselves in a trader's market, people working off the travelers and shipmen from the docks. Voices, animals, the jingling of coins, the rattle of a wheel on the cobblestone pathway, all of the noises seemed to make the group excited. Some of the merchants called out to them, offering their wares, some with foods, some with clothing, and others with jewels or other valuables. Donnic told the group that it would be best not to get anything in this area, as the prices were highly rigged in the dock area.

The group continued to walk through the town, nearly getting hit by a couple of carts whose drivers did not care about the pedestrians in the road. They took a turn at what seemed like a major intersection and headed north towards the area that the crew had recommended as the better part of town. Even though it was quite large and busy, it was a very nice city. The streets were of fine cobblestone. There were trees and plants here and there, beginning to lose their leaves. The great wall around the city cast shadows here and there, but for the most part it was well lit and sunny. After walking a while, they noticed that some of the carts and sellers along the sides of the road began to have lower prices. They continued to walk along, looking for a tavern to get something to eat.

Donnic spotted the sign for the Bull's Horn Inn, a two-story, very rustic looking building. It was near the apparent center of the city, as they saw a sort of commons area down the road a bit, with a large fountain cresting its center. The group walked in, taking in the lively atmosphere. The sweet, strong smell of meat or two roasting over the fire behind the bar, the noise of the travelers, merchants, and seamen enjoying a drink or two; the scene was alive and fun. The four walked up to the bar and Callidus stepped forward, looking for the tender. A short, kind of pudgy man walked behind the bar, carrying two empty mugs. He quickly walked over to a barrel and opened the tap, beginning to fill the mugs with ale.

"Excuse me, sir?" Callidus called to him. The man appeared too busy to hear him. "Sir? Sir?" Callidus called again, a bit louder.

"What? Oh!" the man said in a very gruff, but partially nasal voice. "Some customers. Let me serve these drinks and I'll be right back."

Callidus nodded and motioned the other three to join him. The man eventually made his way back to the bar and greeted the young wizard.

"Hello there and welcome to Two Moons City. My name's Penseval Tranti. My friends just call me Pense."

"Greetings, Pense. My name is Callidus and we're just traveling through on the way to the castle. We smelled the meat over the fire here and it incited our hunger into leading us inside."

"Ah!" he replied with a chuckle. "Well, I'd be pleased to appease your hunger, my friends. I've got some lovely mountain boar over the fire right now. I can get you a plate with a mug of ale for, say, five gold a piece?"

"Sounds good to me. Guys?" With a nod from the other three in response, Callidus pulled out one of the smaller pouches from inside his cloak and took our two ten-piece coins. The man took them with a smile, placing them under the counter, and he walked to the fireplace, taking a wooden plate from a shelf and slicing off four rather hearty portions of meat from the well-roasted boar and laying them on the plate.

"Here you go, four helpings of boar. Take this over to a table and I'll bring you some utensils and some ale."

Callidus took the plate and walked over to a table, the other three joining him. The table already had four wooden bowls on it and a set of candles. They sat down as Pense brought over four mugs of ale and some metal forks. He set the tray down on the table, handing a mug to each person and giving each a two-pronged metal fork, looking more like a skewer than anything else. "Eat up, friends. If you need anything else, please feel free to yell for me."

"We will, thank you, Pense," replied Callidus. The man nodded with a smile and walked away. Callidus stabbed a piece of the meat, placing it in his bowl. The others watched as he attempted to cut a bit of it off using the fork. Finally getting a bite's worth, he placed it in his mouth, smiling at the slightly tough, but still hot, juicy flavor. The others began to eat as well, Callidus pointing out with a chuckle that Donnic took the largest piece.

* * *

After lunch, Callidus and the rest bid farewell to Penseval and they headed eastward toward the castle. They could see the high towers of the castle looming ahead in the distance. They continued to walk for a few more minutes before finally reaching the drawbridge. Before them was a deep moat, no more than ten or eleven feet deep, and filled nearly to the brim with water. It extended on each side to small openings in the outer wall. It was assumable that the moat served mostly as a defense against attack from within the city. A large wooden drawbridge crossed it, giant chains connecting it to two ports on each side of the entrance. Two guards stood on the city side of the moat, two more on the castle side. People were moving across the bridge, to and from the castle. As the group walked onto the drawbridge, they looked around in awe, seeing the huge stones and tall timbers that formed the castle walls. Callidus and Darla's staves clunked on the drawbridge with each drop.

As they walked through the entrance, they could see the inner castle within and the buildings that lined each wall. The rear wall, apparently, was also the rear wall of the castle. The corners of the outer walls were towers, most likely housing more sets of guards.

As they walked toward the main castle, Callidus and the others saw a smithy to one side, a building that had a sign reading "guard barracks," and a well house with some stone bins nearby, among other structures. They reached the entrance to the main castle in no time. Callidus was about to solicit a guard standing in front of the guardhouse for entry, when the door behind the guard opened and a tall, rather old, but still rugged man, dressed in a rather stately outfit with gold trimming and embroidery came out. He quickly walked over to the group, stepping between them and the guard. He gave a few motions to the guard, who nodded in return, and turned back to the group.

"Hello. You are the four to whom we sent word? Yes, right. Come with me."

The very proper, elder voice, as well as the outfit he wore, told them that it would be wise to follow. The group followed behind the man who promptly turned and walked back through the door through which he exited. The four found themselves walking through the guardhouse, down a long hallway that they assumed was to the side, and into a small, dimly candle-lit office-type room. The man they followed said no words as he led them.

"Thank you for coming," said a voice from behind them. The voice came from a similar man who closed the door and lit another candle, setting it on the desk in the room.

"Who are you?" asked Callidus as he, sensing no danger, leaned his staff against the wall. Darla followed.

"My name is Davus Berron. This is Cedrick McCrary," said the first man. "We are the head advisors to the king. We needed to make sure you were not seen."

"Are you the ones who sent for us?"

"Yes," replied Cedrick. "We knew that you were coming. An oracle revealed it, told us of your arrival. I trust you received our letter?"

"Yes, we did," said Callidus, taking the letter from within his robe and setting it on the desk. "But, how did you know where we would be?"

"The clearest point we could predict would be within a mile or so of Kelara Bay. Our diviners could get no closer, so we just sent it there," said Davus, who walked over and sat at the desk.

"Well, do you know who we are?" asked Donnie.

"No, actually. We just know there would be four of you, and a few other things."

"Then," replied Callidus, "let me introduce my party. This is Donnic Turnblade, a swordsman," he said, motioning to Donnic who replied with a nod. "This is Kailynn Belle, who is currently searching out her profession." Kailynn also gave a nod. "My companion in magic here is Darla, Priestess of Agape." She gave a soft smile. "Lastly, I am the leader of this entourage, Callidus Lanstone, sorcerer by trade," he finished, extending his hand to Davus and Cedrick in turn.

"It is a pleasure to meet you, although an ill-timed one," said Cedrick.

"What do you mean, sir?" asked Callidus.

Davus looked to Cedrick then turned back to Callidus. "Well, I wish we had the opportunity to meet on a better note, young friends. I trust you are aware of the guardian spirits within you."

"Well, we know some things, but not too much."

"All right. You do know of the plaguing darkness, correct? Good. The guardian spirits are prophesied to arrive during the reign of the darkness. You four have received the spirits, thus why you are as you are now. I assume you've not all been in the forms you are in now, eh?"

"No, we haven't," replied Donnic.

"And you, young lady, haven't turned at all, have you?" asked Cedrick, turning to Kailynn.

"Unfortunately, no, sir. I have not, yet."

"I see. Callidus, your group will be the only force powerful enough to stop the darkness. The reason we summoned you here is because the darkness has hit home, in the form of a sickness. King Sorrow has fallen ill, fallen to a harsh, debilitating virus that has brought him to blindness, near deafness, and he most recently has become almost completely paralyzed."

"This is terrible, Davus! How did this happen?" asked Callidus.

"That's why we had to get you off to the side. We have discovered that Archpriest Kenather of the cathedral in the city has been slowly sending him this disease. Normally, he is the one we call first to heal our sovereign king. We did this a while ago when somehow our king's food was lightly poisoned. It only gave him some stomach pain, but we suspect that this was somehow done by the Archpriest as well to give him access to the king."

"How do you know he did all this, sir?"

"We suspect that it must be him. He has been acting very strange lately. Some of the guards at the east gate have let him leave the city, often very late at night, with no other companion or guard. This is very strange, as before this started happening, he would hardly ever leave the cathedral, being too devoted to his work. He often stays gone for two or three days at a time, but we know we cannot question why, for fear of our lives and the life of our liege."

"Very strange indeed," remarked Donnic.

"Well, what do you request of us?" asked Callidus.

"We wish you to follow him out of the city tomorrow night. We believe he's been doing something in the Forest of Night, about a half hour outside of town by horse. We think he has someplace set up for himself in Woodsmith Village, so he'll probably be there a couple of days. I wish we could help you in doing this, but we believe that the Archpriest has spies in the castle. He somehow knows when we try to do summon outside help for the king and they get 'misplaced' or whatever else," said Cedrick.

"Yes. The most helpful thing I could do was to arrange for the royal library to let you have access to some of the scrolls in our upper scroll vault," said Davus. "I have eight inscription orbs that I was able to sneak out of the treasury. I keep some personal things in there, so they let me in. They are yours to use. If any of the librarians ask you for some information, tell them that you are the students from the outer province I told them about. You do have a spell tome, correct?" Davus asked as he turned to the stonewall behind him, pulling out part of a stone. He reached in and took out a large bag that rattled as a bag of marbles would. He handed the bag to Callidus, replacing the stone.

"Yes. For the spells, thank you very much. Any other information or assistance you can give us?"

"I'm afraid not, young friends," replied Davus as he stood, walking over to Cedrick. "Do your absolute best to not be discovered by the Archpriest. When you get to Woodsmith Village, it would be in your best interests not to stay in the village. You probably will need to make arrangements to sleep outdoors, at least for the night tomorrow. I've arranged with Penseval Tranti, the owner of the tavern near here, to give you a room tonight."

"Yes, we know him. We had lunch there."

"Good, good. Also, the merchants in the north marketplace have the best materials, but not at the best prices," said Cedrick, walking over to the desk and taking a small piece of paper. "I will give you a note to show to the dealers. They will give you fair prices." He took the quill from the desk, dipping it in the ink and writing out the note. The man handed it to Callidus who noticed that the writing was the same as on the letter. "If you need any armaments, get them at the smithy there. The one in the castle primarily repairs and enchants. It's very rare for him to sell anything to the public."

"Thank you very much, Cedrick, Davus."

"One more thing. Callidus, we wish to meet with you tonight. If you are to be the leader of this group, there is much you need to know. Come alone to the outer gate. If the drawbridge is up, we couldn't make it. If it is down, come inside," said Davus.

"Yes, of course. Thank you both."

The four of them left the inner castle, walking out to the main courtyard. "All right. What's the plan, Calli?" asked Darla.

"Well, the two of us need to go to the library and get the spells. Donnic, Kailynn, the two of you go to the marketplace. How much gold do you have, Donnic?"

"I've got about two hundred," he replied.

"I've got a hundred, myself," said Kailynn.

"Okay. Take my pouch, as well," he said, taking it from his belt and tossing it over. "There's three hundred in it. Darla's got the rest of the gold in that orb bag."

"I'd like to see if there are any weapons I could use there," said Kailynn.

"All right. As far as weapons goes, get me a long dagger. I can't use a sword. I guess because it hampers my casting ability," said Callidus.

"Okay. What else?" asked Donnic.

"Get a large bag to use to carry some things and four or five more pouches, a bit larger than the ones we've got, the three coin pouches and one orb bag," said Callidus. "Also, I'd like a pair of gloves and get a length of whatever material you can that would make good tents, bedrolls, etc. A couple of blankets, as well. Do any of us know how to sew? I don't."

"I do," said Kailynn. "My grandmother taught me how."

"Okay. What else do we need?" asked Callidus.

Donnic motioned to his clothes, saying, "I'm going to look for some pieces of armor to better equip myself. Either of you want any armor?"

"No, we can't use it," replied Darla. "The book, when it was still full, said it also interferes with our casting ability. Try and get some potions for healing and whatnot. Oh, and a few empty vials, so I can try out the herbs book."

"Okay. I'll see what I can get. Anything else?"

"I don't think so. We can get our food supply before we leave tomorrow," said Callidus.

"Gotcha. We'll get started on that; you two get to the library."

Callidus and Darla nodded and waved them goodbye. The other two turned and walked out of the courtyard. "I need to see if I can get the enchantment on my staff recharged before we leave. Think we could get the castle smith to do it?"

"Possibly. Let's get on into the library first. I do believe it's in that tower there."

"What can I do for you, young lad?" the old woman asked, not bothering to look up from the parchment she was reading. Her voice was scratchy, high-pitched, and almost aggravating to the ear, very loud as almost a sign of hearing loss. She sat at a wooden desk in the midst of the large, stone room. There were several stone bookcases all around, filled with very old volumes of one thing or another. There were scroll racks here and there as well.

"We're the students Davus told you about?"

"I do not remember any students, young man," the woman said, rather loudly, and continued to eye the papers over on her desk.

"Are you certain? We're from the magic school...from the outer province? Here to use the scroll vault?"

"As I've already told you, I do not know of any students from a magic school. Now, you can feel free to use the rest of the library at your disposal, otherwise, leave. I'm quite busy and have no time to deal with 'students' from a magic school."

Callidus turned to Darla, shrugging.

"I swear," the woman mumbled to herself, though not all too quietly, "they'll let anyone just walk into a regal library such as this. Now, let's see. Magistrate from winter province to join us at sunrise tomorrow, yes, yes…"

"What are we going to do?" asked Callidus.

"I don't know," said Darla.

"Davus will be sending the blacksmith to receive the new sword enchantment for the castle guard. Students from a magic school coming to use the vault. Another magistrate…" The woman paused for a second.

Callidus looked at the woman, arching a brow.

"Oh dear…" She looked up at the two young people. "Very sorry. Didn't read that letter, sorry indeed. The upper vault is just down that hall and to your left. Stay out of the lower vault, students can't handle that magic."

Callidus turned to Darla and shrugged once more. The two of them walked down the hall the woman motioned to and found a doorway with a wooden plaque next to it reading "Upper Vault." The two walked in, seeing row after row of scroll racks on stands, on the walls, etc.

"Well, what should we get?" asked Darla, walking around, glancing at racks but not yet touching them.

"Hmm. I'm not sure. We've both got four orbs to use, so we'd better make them count," he replied, walking around as well.

"All right. I'll try and find something useful in my range of ability. How will we know which ones we can use and which ones we can't?"

"I'm not sure. I guess we…" He stopped as he passed his hand over a scroll case and the scrolls contained within faintly glowed. "I think that's how we know. Come here and try this."

She walked over and waved her hand over the same case, noticing that nothing happened. "I believe so as well," she said with a chuckle. She walked to some other cases, trying the same until she found a section that glowed for her. "I think all those are yours and all these are mine."

Callidus nodded and started to examine the scrolls. He picked one up, seeing that they were all mostly wound around finely carved wooden rods with ornate ends. He unrolled it a bit, reading a bit of the text. "'A ward to keep a fly from stew...' I don't think so."

Darla picked up a scroll, unrolling it, and reading, "'To keep a splinter from your forefinger...' Not helpful."

The two continued to sift through the spells, finding many that were of no use to them whatsoever. Darla found a spell to cast a ward over food to keep it from spoiling and took it off the rack, placing it under her arm. She assumed it wouldn't hold for very long, but it would help nonetheless. Adjacent to it, she found another ward to keep bugs and small animals away from a group of people. That would be greatly helpful if they had to sleep outdoors.

After much more looking, she also discovered a spell to create confusion in someone's mind. That would work wonders if they ran into problems. She continued to look, carrying the scrolls with her as she went.

Callidus searched the scrolls that would glow for him for quite some time, finding some spells that would just seem to be very ineffective for his purposes. He found some that could make hammers and nails stronger, wonderful for a blacksmith or carpenter, not for him. He found others that would change the color of clothing or put flowers on any hat, but those would be more suited for a tailor.

He eventually came across a spell to blind a person temporarily, which he saw use in. He took that one down and continued to search.

"Having any luck, Calli?" asked Darla as she sat down her scrolls on a table near the center of the room.

"Unfortunately, no. I've found a blindness spell, but that's about it. What did you find?"

"I found a food preservation ward, a confusion spell, and a bug and beastie ward. I thought I'd come over and help you look."

"Thanks. Just glad that you're on a roll," he said with a chuckle.

Her face turned into a mock scowl as she said, "Ooh, very bad.

Very, very bad."

He chuckled and continued to sift through the scrolls. He unrolled one, reading, "'To give a scent of lily to the wind...' Don't think so. There aren't many helpful spells here. At least, not in my range."

"I know. Well, let me have three of the orbs and I'll start copying these spells."

"All right," he said, taking the orb pouch from his belt. He took out a handful of orbs, counting four in his hand, and gave them all to her except one. As he held the orb over the bag and was about to drop it, he suddenly sneezed, the orb dropping from his hand and rolling away. "Oh no! We've got to catch it!"

The orb rolled under several scroll cases, heading toward a wall. He dashed around the scroll racks, eventually reaching the wall just in time to see the orb roll straight through it! It made sounds of clunking down a flight of stairs. "What the..." Callidus walked forward, attempting to press his hand against the wall but finding that it too passed through it. "This must be a secret passage! Come on!"

The two followed the sound of the clunking orb down a long, winding spiral staircase, lit only by a few sparse torches here and there. They eventually reached the bottom and, to their surprise, found themselves in the lower vault! Before them spread hundreds and hundreds of scroll cases, bookcases, etc. Magical power seemed to emanate throughout the vault, flowing from each potent spell. Callidus saw the orb roll under a scroll case and eventually heard it clink against something. He followed the sound and eventually found himself at a scroll case. The orb had clinked against its leg and rested there.

He bent down to pick up the orb and, upon rising, he began to glance around the vault.

"Callidus, I think we should probably go..."

"What kind of spells are these, Darla?" he asked, almost not even hearing her. He waved his hand over one of the scrolls on the rack facing Darla and saw no activity. He took one and unrolled it, saying, "Wow, Darla! Listen to this! 'An invocation to tear a chasm in the ground...' This is powerful stuff."

Darla also picked up a spell, beginning to be taken in by the power that seemed to flow through the room. "My God, listen to this, 'To sever the spirit from a body and coerce it to the void...' How horrible...these are definitely in your genre. A priestess of light would never do this."

Callidus turned around to the rack at which his orb had landed. As he reached for a spell, three of the scrolls on the rack began to glow. "Darla—come over here..." He passed his hand over them once more, seeing them start to illuminate. "This must be why the orb landed here..."

"Wow.... Think we could get any of these spells?"

"Maybe. As long as we don't let on to the librarian, she might not find out," he said, taking a scroll from the case. "Well, let's see what we have here. 'A minor manipulation of the power of water...' Interesting."

Darla took one from the case, reading aloud, "Interesting. 'A minor manipulation of the power of the earth.' Hmm."

Callidus took another as well, saying, "This last one follows the same pattern. 'A minor manipulation of the power of the air...' The question is: which one do I pick?"

"Well, read the scroll a little further, and see what it says."

He unrolled the air scroll a bit further and found somewhat of a list of examples of what the spell could do. Apparently, an air manipulation could be anything from causing a breeze to blow to changing the temperature of the air around something. A bit of electricity seemed to be included, but not much more than creating some sparks, things like that.

Darla reread the earth scroll, seeing that it gave abilities such as creating balls of dirt or rock to heave at something, causing a very minor tremor in the ground, etc.

Callidus placed the air scroll down and took the water scroll. He read that it would, of course, produce water, create very minor rain, make mud puddles at someone's feet, and other things of that nature.

"Well, which one will it be?" asked Darla.

"Why not all three? I've got three orbs, and I could certainly use all three spells. Why not?"

"I guess so. Grab the scrolls and let's start copying. Is there any place to do it?"

"I saw a table over by the door," Callidus replied. "Dash upstairs and grab your scrolls and let's do this before anyone sees us. I left that blindness scroll with the ones you found."

Darla turned and walked toward the door. As she went, her hand absently waved over the top of one of the racks and a single scroll illuminated briefly. She did not even notice until Callidus stopped her. "Darla, look. Go back a couple of scroll racks and do the hand thing."

She backed up a bit, finding herself at the one he directed to and waved her hand over the top. The same, single scroll lit up. She took it up and unrolled it. "Here's another element, but it's mine. 'A minor manipulation of power of light…' It will allow me to create light in small amounts, illuminate certain things, and form feasible balls of light, apparently, among other things."

"Good, that will be useful."

Darla picked up the scroll and quickly walked upstairs, obtaining the rest of the scrolls before anyone saw her.

They began the process of copying the scrolls to the tome and, after about an hour's time, they were finished. Through further reading, they discovered that the manipulations could be used no more than "twice by each rise of the sun." The other spells did not give any sort of timing hints, so they would need to be found through use.

"We'd better leave. That librarian might have some way of knowing what we did," said Callidus. Darla agreed.

The two walked up to the main library and headed toward the door, trying to avoid the eye of the librarian.

Donnic and Kailynn walked through the portcullis, heading across the drawbridge and into the main city. They turned in the direction of the marketplace and started down the cobblestone road. The sounds of the marketplace soon hit their ears; people shouting out to sell their wares, customers and vendors bickering over the price of this and that, noises from the livestock that were being sold, etc.

"Let's see, what all are we supposed to get again?" asked Kailynn.

"Hmm. Okay, Chris…" He chuckled and corrected himself. "Callidus, I mean, said to get some pouches, one large bag, some blankets…oh, what else?"

"The tent material. He also wanted some gloves. Darla wanted some potions and some empty vials. And the dagger, too."

Donnic nodded. They headed into the main marketplace and began to look around. After a bit of looking, Kailynn found the mercer's shop where they bought enough material to make four bedrolls and two tents, with about four yards extra to spare. The material was a light but durable cloth, similar to burlap but a bit softer. As was expected, the shopkeeper was trying to charge a lot more than what it was worth, but the note from Davus lowered the price significantly. It seemed capitalism wasn't just an earthen ideal. They also purchased a couple of needles and some strong thread to sew the items with. Kailynn had learned how to sew from her grandmother, so she would be able to assemble the cloth into its useful final forms.

Through a bit more browsing, they came to the draper's shop. Donnic purchased the four pouches Callidus had asked for, giving one to Kailynn and placing another on his belt. Kailynn placed hers on her belt as well. Donnic also bought a large bag, probably about five feet deep and a couple of feet wide. He placed the pouches inside as well as the material from the mercer. Kailynn obtained a pair of wrist-buttoned gloves, a dark blue that would just about match Callidus' robes. The blankets were found here as well.

Nearby, they found an apothecary where they bought about five empty vials, looking like each wouldn't hold more than a few ounces. Their shelves were stocked with curatives and potions, but not knowing which to get, they decided to not get any at the moment, but to let Darla come back later and decide.

They headed next to the smithy where they saw the blacksmith working over a hot fire. The building was encased in a waist-high fence topped by a shed roof. The back wall had a door that was currently shut. Donnic picked up a dagger for Callidus, about 9 inches long hilt to tip. Kailynn picked up a bow and began to examine it a bit as Donnic went to talk to the smithy about his own equipment.

"Hello there, sir. Can you suit me up in some traveling armor?"

"Why, of course young man. I've got some things you can purchase. Come inside," he said, leading him towards the door. He stopped and looked toward Kailynn, saying, "You with this lad?"

"Yes, sir."

"Watch the merchandise. If there's any trouble, you yell for me, and don't try and take anything, got it?"

"Of course, sir," she replied, continuing to look at the bow.

The blacksmith led him into the storage room behind the smithy. There were shelves full of various weaponry, armor, and other bits and pieces, as well as some wooden bins full of pieces of metal, cloth, and leather. There was a bit of wood stacked up against one wall, most likely for the fire.

"What kind of activity are you planning on using this armor for?" asked the blacksmith.

Donnic thought for a second then said, "Well, me and my friends are going to be doing some traveling shortly and I'm the protector of the group, so I need to be able to withstand a fight if we encounter a gang of ruffians or something."

"Ah, so you want something light, but durable? How about some hard leather?" the blacksmith asked, walking over to a shelf of pieces made from the material.

"That sounds good. What all do I need?" he asked, looking the pieces over.

"Well, let's start with the basics. First, you'll need some body armor." He took from the shelf a studded leather jerkin, looking almost like a large vest. It strapped at the shoulder and laced on each side. Its hardened surface was covered in metal studs, providing a bit of extra protection. "Try this on. Put it on over your clothes for now."

Donnic put on the jerkin, strapping it at the shoulders, not bothering to lace the sides. He moved around a bit, stretching his arms, bending around, etc. "I like this. It's not too heavy, and it seems like it'll work well."

"Good. Let's see here. Ah, you'll want some gauntlets." He took down a pair of leather gauntlets that were just longer than the wrist. Donnic slipped them on his hands and wiggled his fingers. He unsheathed his sword and twisted it around a bit. "Do you have a set that is a little more flexible in the fingers?" he asked, removing them and giving them back to the smith.

The blacksmith took them and placed them back on the shelf, looking through the few pairs he had there. He took another one that appeared to be of a bit thinner leather. These extended nearly to the elbow. "Try these."

Donnic put them on, repeating the process. He found he was better able to maneuver in this pair and nodded to the man.

"The boots you're wearing now won't do you much good around the legs. Let's get you in some bracers." He took down a pair of metal bracers, looking similar to boots, but fitted with metal plates to protect the shins, a mesh of metal at the knee with a bit of a hinge to allow the joint to move, and additional plates for the upper leg.

Donnic slipped out of his boots and slipped into the bracers. "Good fit. They'll do."

"I think that's about all you'll really need. Let me get you a set of underclothes to wear with this armor. It'll do you good to have them anyways, as it's soon to get rather cold outside, and it'll help keep you warm. It also will prevent chafing and will give you a bit more impact buffering."

He walked over to another shelf and took down a pair of leggings designed to go under the pants, as well as an undertunic, padded a bit and made to go underneath the usual tunic. It looked as if it could stand alone, as well. "This should be about all you'll need. If you think of anything else you'd like, I'll be glad to suit you up."

"Thank you very much. How much for all of this?" he asked as the two walked back outside.

"Well, let's see. For the whole get up, let's say, two hundred gold?"

"All right, it's a deal." Donnic took twenty ten-piece coins from his pouch and handed them to the blacksmith. He walked over to Kailynn and showed off his armor.

Kailynn had picked up an arrow from a quiver hanging inside the shed. As she placed it at the bow, she noticed a slight bump at her side. She turned to see a short, thin man dashing away from her. She looked to her belt and noticed that her pouch was gone.

"Hey miss, that guy—," someone nearby began to say.

She shouted, "Hey, stop! Thief!" Donnic turned and was about to chase after him when he saw that Kailynn had raised the bow and was pulling back the arrow. When she let it fly, the same images and sounds rushed through her head as the arrow seemed to sail right between each of the numerous people in its path. The man had but a few seconds to look back before the arrow nailed him in the shin. He cried out in pain and dropped like a rock.

A crowd gathered around the man as a few town guards stepped out of the woodwork. Kailynn, shaking off the foreboding image of the eyes, and Donnic now stood above the man, Kailynn now standing nearly six feet head to toe. Her body was now very lithe and her hair, still fiery red, was now tied behind her in a long ponytail. The man looked up at her in a bit of dismay, but nevertheless cringed as his leg throbbed.

"What's going on here, young lady?" asked one of the guards, two others waiting behind him.

"This man stole my coin purse."

"Have you any proof?"

She reached down and took her pouch from within the man's coat. "Here's the purse."

"And I saw him take it," said a man who stepped up. "I was walking towards the smithy when the guy bumped into her and ran." The smith stepped up beside him as well.

"Thank you, sir," said Kailynn, nodding to the man.

"That's that, then,' said the guard, nodding to one of the ones behind him. "Take him to the guardhouse and get him doctored up."

"Yes, sir." The guard picked the man up, a small shout of pain following.

"Wait a second. Let me look at him," said the first guard. He took a good look at the man, then said, "Why, this is the pickpocket who's been working all over town! We've been after him all week. Young lady, you just caught a great thief."

Kailynn blushed a bit and smiled. "Thank you, sir."

The guard waved him away and turned back to Kailynn. "Some of our best archers wouldn't have been able to time that so perfectly. Where on earth did you learn the bow so well?"

"Well, it's," she paused with a chuckle, "just natural talent, I guess."

The man chuckled himself and turned to the smithy, saying, "Give this woman your best bow and charge it to the guard. Don't cheat her on arrows either."

"Yes, of course, right away," said the blacksmith, taking the bow she had and walking back to the smithy.

"What's your name, miss?" asked the guard.

"Kailynn Belle, sir."

"Kailynn, you've got a position on the town guard anytime you want."

"Thank you, sir. We're just passing through, but I'll remember it if I'm back this way."

"You do that, Miss Belle," the guard said. He shook Donnic's hand, saying, "If this girl's traveling with you, you've got quite an asset."

Donnic nodded, shaking the man's hand in return.

"Let's go," said the guard, turning to his other comrade, the two walking away.

"We're four for four. Welcome to the team," said Donnic, giving her a big hug.

"Here you go, miss, the best bow I have." They turned to see the smithy standing behind them, holding a very nice, black composite bow and a full quiver of very fine arrows.

"Thank you, sir. Thank you very much," she replied.

"There are some extra strings and some string wax as well, just look in the quiver."

"Thanks for all your help, sir," said Donnic, shaking the man's work-worn hand.

"Do we have everything?" asked Kailynn, removing her cloak and strapping the quiver and bow to her back. She tied the cloak around her waist, as she was now wearing black leather pants, long boots, with a long-sleeved, brown cotton tunic, covered by a forest green tunic-vest.

"I think so. How much did all that cost?"

Kailynn started to figure it up, saying, "Well, let's see. We spent a hundred and twenty at the mercer, fifty at the draper, and two hundred thirty five at the blacksmith. So that's…"

Donnic was adding in his head as she spoke and said, "That should be four hundred and five."

"That sounds about right. Well, let's go back to the castle."

Callidus and Darla walked over to the blacksmith's shed, seeing a rather short, fairly muscular, but rotund man working over the fire. "Hello, sir. I was wondering—"

"Put it in the bin," the man interrupted, not looking up from the piece of plate armor he was working on. "I'll get to it later. 50 for swords, 50 for armor, 30 for helmets and shields."

"No, sir, I don't need a repair."

"What is it, then? Can't you see I'm—" The man stopped as he looked up and saw the staff in Callidus' hand. "Why, that looks like the staff I made for Andrepate several years ago."

"Was it enchanted with fire, for a trip in the northern provinces?" Callidus asked, handing it to him to inspect.

"It certainly was! Well, what do you know? Does the fire still work?" he asked, taking the staff from Callidus' hands and looking it over.

"Barely. It's dwindled down to little more than a torch."

"Ah! I see. Well, what do you need from me?"

"I'd like to get the enchantment recharged, if you can."

"Oh, well, I'm quite sorry, but I've not had that enchantment, Firebare it was called, I've not had it since that very staff. I have other enchantments, if you'd like to see them."

"Well, if I can't get this enchantment, I might as well get a new one. Let's see what you have."

The man nodded and walked over one of the walls. He whispered a few words to the lock on a long wooden box, at least three feet in length. The lock popped open and, as the man opened it, the box revealed an array of casting orbs varied in color and size. Callidus and Darla walked over, looking at the maybe thirty or forty orbs lined up in two rows.

"Wow, look at all those, Callidus!" Darla exclaimed.

"They're pretty much all equipment enchantments. I mostly only do repairs and enchantments. I also sell repair orbs to the men to use on the field. Of course, my hammer makes a big difference," he said with a chuckle.

"Well, what staff enchantments do you have?" asked Callidus.

He counted out about five orbs and said, "These orbs are for staves. I've got two orbs for the Solidarity enchantment, makes your staff nearly unbreakable. I've got one called Sombnamb, which gives your staff the ability to put someone to sleep when you strike them. However, it's a very random effect, doesn't work all the time."

"Hmm. What else do you have?" asked Callidus, pondering the choices.

"Well, I've got two more orbs and they're both for the Callback enchantment. It calls the staff to your hand from wherever it may be, similar to the enchantments that are usually placed on spell tomes. Don't think it can be used more than twenty or thirty yards away, though."

"That would be really useful for both of us, Callidus," said Darla. She turned to the blacksmith after Callidus nodded in agreement and asked, "Can you enchant both our staves with that?"

"I do believe so. But," he said, turning to Callidus, "the fire

enchantment on your staff will be erased if I put a new one on."
Callidus nodded and handed the man his staff. "Go ahead. How
much for both of our staves?"
"Well, since this is one of my staves, I won't charge you for it.
And for hers, let's say fifty gold?"
Darla nodded and reached into the orb bag, now holding only
gold, and took out five of the larger coins. She handed him her staff
as well and the man set them both against the wall.
"I'll get started on them right now. Come back in, say, fifteen
minutes?"

"Callidus, Darla!" They turned to see Donnic who had called out
from the courtyard entrance. Darla and Kailynn embraced in a hug
when Darla noticed that she had changed. Chris also hugged her and
congratulated her on her metamorphosis.
"Good to know that we have the whole team. Kailynn, you're our
ranger. You've found yourself a bow, I see."
"Yes, and you should have seen me! This guy stole my pouch
while I was looking at a bow, so I grabbed an arrow and shot him dead
in the leg, maybe at fifty yards, maybe a hundred. There had to be
thirty or more people in the way, too, but I just seemed to know just
the right moment to fire."
"Wonderful, Kailynn! Your skills will come in handy, no doubt,"
said Darla.
"All right. Did you get everything?"
"Yeah, here's your dagger," said Donnie, taking it from his belt
and handing it to him.
"Thanks," he said, slipping it into a secret fold within his robe.
"Isn't that going to rip your robe?" asked Kailynn
"No, sorcerer's robes are very strong. They have to be as we can't
wear armor."
"Oh, and here's your gloves as well," said Kailynn, taking them
from the bag. She also handed Darla her vials.
"Good, thanks." Callidus placed them on each hand, seeing that
each went a couple inches up his wrist then buttoned. He buttoned

them and continued. "Okay, well, we need to get back to the inn and get organized. The blacksmith is enchanting our staves; they should be about ready now. Anything else we need to do in town?"

The three shook their heads. Callidus walked over to the smithy and took the newly enchanted staves from him with, giving him thanks, and walked back over. He handed Darla her staff and the four walked back toward the inn.

As the four began to walk, a tall figure stepped out of a building just ahead of them, wearing a bright, rather ornate white robe bearing the symbol of the sun and the two moons. The man began walk in the direction of the four and noticed them, stopping as they approached.

"Good afternoon to you. I do believe we have not met. Are you newcomers to our town?" asked the robed figure. His gray hair and slightly aged face was kept by a warm smile.

"Why yes, sir, we are. We have stopped here on our way to complete some business," replied Callidus.

"Ah, then let me introduce myself. I am Archpriest Kenather of the Temple of Agape at Two Moons. I see you are a priestess, young lass."

A sudden expression of shock and fear came across the girls' faces as the archpriest introduced himself. The two guys exchanged looks.

"Is something the matter? Are you in need of healing?" asked the still smiling archpriest, noticing the sudden change in their countenances.

"No, no. I think it might just be—" Kailynn said, pausing, then continued. "It's probably what we had for breakfast. Callidus, I think we should probably get back to the inn. I feel like lying down"

"Me too," said Darla.

"Well, I will pray that your stomachs are settled. If you need healing, please find me at the temple. I am always willing to help an Agape sister and her companions," he said, the smile on his face remaining steady.

"Thank you," replied Darla.

"Oh, by the way, please drop by some time and we can discuss the teachings, if you'd like."

Darla nodded and the group walked away from him rather hurriedly. He continued along his way, smiling almost forcedly as he walked.

"He seemed like a nice guy but there was just something creepy about him," said Kailynn.

"You're right. I don't like him. We definitely need to avoid another meeting with him," said Donnic.

"And I'm definitely not going to go discuss squat with him," said Darla, stepping closer to Callidus. "He just freaks me out."

"Care to take a walk with me before you go, Callidus?"

Callidus looked up at hearing his name and saw Darla standing above him, wearing her blouse and pants, but not in her clerical robe. He was seated at a table in the inn, going over the maps of the area again. He was working by lamplight now, as the sun had begun to set. "Oh! hello there, Darla. Sure, let me just pack all these up." Callidus rolled up the maps and slipped them inside a bag Kailynn had made to hold scrolls and other papers. She had been hard at work all day with Darla and Donnic helping as much as they could. Callidus had been at work studying the maps of the area surrounding the Forest of Night. It seemed that there would be a couple of routes they could take to avoid the Archpriest yet still reach the Forest of Night around the same time.

Callidus stood up, the folds of his robe falling around his legs. He noticed Kailynn who had followed Darla down. "Can you put this back in my room?"

"Yes of course. Donnie—Donnic, I mean, is up there cutting a bit more of the material. I came down to get a drink," Kailynn replied.

"Wonderful. How are we coming along?"

"Well, we lost about half a yard of the fabric thanks to a mistaken cut by Mr. Turnblade. I'll keep it to reuse somehow, though. We've gotten one of the bedrolls and one tent done. He's got the material cut for another bedroll and is cutting for another tent now. It wasn't easy, but Pense let me buy two of his sheets for a few gold to make some patterns."

"Good, good. I want to thank you for all your hard work. We definitely wouldn't be ready tomorrow night if we didn't have you." Kailynn blushed a bit and smiled with a nod. "It was nothing. Just doing my part for us." She took the scroll case from his hand. "We should have everything done with us working a bit more tonight, then more tomorrow morning and afternoon."

"Good. All right, well, Darla will be back shortly. We're going to take a walk then I'm going to go to the castle to see Cedrick and Davus."

Kailynn nodded and Callidus and Darla walked outside. The chill of the night air hit them as they left the warmth of the inn's fire and Darla shivered a bit. Callidus smiled to her softly and loosened the belt on his robe, pulling it over enough so that Darla snuggled up to his side as he wrapped the robe and his arm around her. She smiled up to him and rested her head against his shoulder as they walked.

"It is a bit chilly out here tonight, isn't it?" asked Callidus.

"Yes, I definitely won't forget my robe again," she replied with a mischievous giggle. He grinned back to her as they walked through the town. As the sun started to set, people started to wrap up their business, shutting down their stands and heading into their homes.

"It is warm in your arms, however," said Darla, sighing sweetly.

Callidus smiled as they walked along. The sky was now in its final stage of orange before the night sky would become apparent. "Tomorrow may be the first time I really have to test my leadership. It's going to be very dangerous…" He trailed off as he thought about what might happen to them, to her.

"I'm certain things will go well. I feel safe knowing that you're leading us. I know anything could happen, but I'm not afraid. A bit nervous, perhaps, but not afraid, knowing that you care about me enough that you would…lay down your life for me."

"That I would, Darla. I care about you a lot. Donnie's like a brother to me. Catie's like a sister. You're…more than that."

The two had continued to walk, eventually reaching the fountain in the town square. They stood looking into it as it reflected the gaze of the larger of the moons, glimmering softly.

"What am I, Chris? To you?"

"You're...you're very dear to me, Darla," he said, taking his robe from his own shoulder and placing it around hers. He looked into her eyes, saying, "I feel as though we've known each other for lifetimes upon lifetimes. There's just something about you, about your smile that makes *me* want to smile." He did smile now as he slowly leaned toward her.

She looked into his eyes, seeing that same familiar sparkle within them. Her smile came with a blush at his remark. "Chris...is there something between—"

She was interrupted with the answer to her question as he softly pressed his lips against hers. He took her into his arms tenderly as he kissed her. She melted into them, wrapping hers about his neck. The kiss seemed to last for ages, sheltered in the moonlight, creating within her a kind of warmth that the robe could not provide. As he released the tender kiss, his heart was pounding. Only hers could have been more excited as they gazed into each other's eyes.

A flicker of the moonlight off the rippling fountain, though, brought her back to reality as she realized how late it was getting. She whispered through her smile, "You'd better get going. Don't want to stand Davus and Cedrick up."

He looked to the now dark sapphire sky and nodded. They turned, walking back to the inn, his arm still around her. She pulled the robe around them both this time until they reached the tavern. She stepped in the doorway and turned to face him. With a soft smile, she leaned up to his ear and whispered, "We'll talk later." She removed the robe from around her shoulders and wrapped it back onto his, tying the belt at his waist.

He smiled to her and nodded, lifting the hood on his robe. He waved his hand, calling his staff into it and walked down the road, turning to look back at Darla who was leaning against the doorframe, gazing after him. Light filled the city from the moons above, cascading shadows from the walls and buildings. The stars shone brightly against the royal blue backdrop.

Eventually he found himself at the castle, drawbridge down. He stepped up onto it, lifting his staff so as to not make noise. He approached the portcullis but noticed that there were no guards on duty. *Must have been arranged by Davus and Cedrick*, he thought. He looked around and, not seeing anyone nearby, leaned on his staff to wait.

"Glad that you could make it," said a voice from nowhere. Suddenly, he saw Davus step out from the shadows of the castle wall.

"Nice trick, my friend. Are we going inside?"

"Yes, let me just—" He was interrupted as the crackle of a leaf was heard. Davus turned, seeing no one there. Callidus also looked around, but didn't see anything either. "Very peculiar," said Davus, turning back toward Callidus. "I really think we should get inside, I'm not sure if—"

Suddenly, a sharp whirr sounded and Davus cried out, clutching his side. Two men stepped out from the shadows to their side, one holding a dagger in each hand, the other holding only one. Davus clutched the dagger and pulled it from his side, shouting to Callidus, "Run! Run! You cannot be killed! You must—" One of the men quickly kicked him hard in the leg, causing him to drop.

Callidus shouted, "No!" He threw up his hands, dropping his staff, as one of them turned toward him, and quickly shouted a few arcane words, light flashing from his hand.

The man clutched his eyes, screaming, "Oh God, I can't see!" He dropped to his knees, his hands pressed to his face. Callidus quickly called back his staff and gave the man a swift crack against the side of his head. The man was knocked over, unconscious and bleeding.

Callidus suddenly remembered the other man, just in time to turn toward him as the assailant brought his dagger down against Callidus' left arm, slashing deeply. He cried out in pain, a blur flashing over his eyes, and dropped his staff. The man was about to lunge again when suddenly the bones of his feet cracked apart. He screamed sharply and fell to the ground. Callidus faintly saw that Davus had just lowered his glowing hand. When Callidus had recovered enough, he called his staff into his right hand and swung it hard enough to hit the assailant across the face, knocking him out as well. He maneuvered over the men, still clutching the wound of his arm, which was bleeding heavily, and knelt beside Davus. There was a pool of blood beneath the man.

"Boy...you cannot let them stop you...you are too important. Run...run away from here, Cedrick will...find you..."

"Davus, no! You can't die! Please, we still need you! I can get help, I," he paused, feeling a deep shot of pain from his arm.

"Go now, Callidus! Go...you must...you..." Davus ceased his words, taking a pained, roughened breath and closing his eyes. His head dropped onto the cold, hard ground and, as his breath released, Callidus knew his time was over.

Callidus shouted, "Guards! Guards!" He stood up suddenly, however, clutching his arm again, and started to stumble towards the inn, knowing that if he was found, there could be trouble. He eventually stumbled into the inn, collapsing on the floor. He cried out in pain and could hear the scuffle of feet, but his eyes blurred as he felt his arm grow cold and numb. He cried out once more, but the sounds fell away.

9

Reflection of the Forest

Callidus' eyes opened to the bright sun shining through his bedroom window. For a moment, he thought that he was back at home, waking up to get ready for school. A twinge of pain in his arm, however, brought him back to the inn.

"Good, you're awake," said Darla, walking over to his side.

"How long have I been asleep?" he said, feeling a bit of soreness in his jaw.

"Since we found you yesterday. It's almost noon now. How are you feeling?"

Callidus tried to sit up, saying, "My arm...it's throbbing."

Darla helped him get to a sitting position and he saw that he was indeed lying in his room at the inn. He saw a bowl of water and a blood soaked towel next to it. His arm was wrapped tightly in a bit of bandage. There was a blanket in a chair in the room. "Have...you been watching over me?"

"Of course. I cast the healing spell over you as soon as we found you," she said, moving a bit closer to take his right hand comfortingly. "And I needed to stay nearby to cast it again once it came back, so I offered to watch over you. It seemed to come to me quicker as I had need of it. I got a few hours of sleep, so don't worry about it."

Callidus looked at his arm then looked to her, smiling at her soft, delicate face. She had really stayed with him all night, making sure he was all right. "Thank you, Darla. Please, help me up." Darla helped him get to his feet. "Tell me, what happened last night...after I ran?"

The two walked out the door and started down the stairs. "Well, a messenger came to us this morning, asking for you. Of course, you were still asleep, but Donnic took the message. It said only that the assassins' daggers were a bit poisoned and the poison was meant to hit a major organ to cause the most damage. That's why Davus died. It just caused you to fall unconscious."

"So, Davus really is dead?"

"Yes, I'm afraid so. But regardless, the guards caught the assassins and took them—"

"Callidus!" He turned to see Kailynn rushing toward him.

"Whoa! The arm! The arm," he shouted, warning her.

She chuckled and lightly hugged his right side, saying, "I'm glad to see you're all right. You gave us quite a scare!"

"Sorry about that. Those guys...gave me quite a scare, too..."

Darla walked him over to a table, sitting beside him and wrapping her arms around his right arm. Kailynn sat across from them. "I should be able to cast the healing spell again within the hour. I think that'll basically rid the wound from you. The wound is almost sealed and it has stopped bleeding for the most part," she said, lightly patting his good arm. "Tell us what happened last night."

"Well, after I dropped you off here, I went to meet Davus just like I was supposed to. Only, when I got there, the assassins were waiting for us as well. Kenather must have found out about me. I got there and Davus hadn't said probably two things before a dagger flew out of nowhere and struck him in the side," he said, sighing a bit. "Next thing you know, I've blinded one of the guys and the other stabbed me." He motioned to his arm. "I was able to knock one of them a good one, but the other one would have definitely struck me again had it not been for Davus' help. I'm not quite sure what he did, but he cast something and the guy dropped like a rock."

"I would assume you left shortly after," said Kailynn.

"Yes. I figured that it would have drawn a lot of unneeded

133

attention to me to be found there. I called for the guards and took off."

"Well, I'm just glad you're safe," said Darla, smiling to him softly.

"Me too," added Kailynn.

"Where's Don?" asked Callidus.

"He went to try and get some more information. He's lying low, though. Don't worry," said Kailynn, smiling as well.

"Thank you, both of you," he said, leaning on Darla a bit as he leaned back in his chair.

"Did you really fight off both of those men, Callidus?" asked Darla.

"Yes, but I really couldn't have done it without Davus. Though…I was a bit surprised at how strong my body is. I can remember having no strength hardly at all in my former body."

Darla looked up at him, smiling softly. *How brave*, she thought. *He could have been killed, but he fought them off trying to save his and Davus' life.* Suddenly, the words to the spell came back into her mind again. "Here, it's time for another healing."

Callidus nodded and laid his arm out on the table. Darla slowly unwrapped the bandages, a bit of stinging was felt by Callidus as the blood-soaked cloth came off. Kailynn turned her head, not liking at all the sight of such things. Darla finished removing the bandages, revealing a red scar, a few inches long, blood dried on each side. She waved her hands over it and began chanting. The pure, healing light began to trickle into the almost completely healed wound. Within moments, the wound was sealed, leaving only the dried blood and a faintly noticeable bit of scar.

"How does that feel?" asked Darla.

"Better, still a bit sore, but better," he replied. "I'm quite hungry, though. Think we could go grab something to eat?"

"Sure, Callidus. Want me to get you something from the bar?" asked Darla.

"No, I want something different. Let's see if there are any other places in town to eat."

"You two go on ahead," said Kailynn. "I've got to make sure the preparations are set for tonight. I'm going to try and round up some horses to travel with. We're still going, aren't we?"

"Yes, of course. Can't let something little like this delay us," he replied, with a chuckle. With that, Darla and Callidus stood up and walked out the door, Darla's arm still wrapped around his.

They found themselves at a little place in town, almost a Mom-and-Pop style diner. Only the sun that streamed in through the windows provided the quaint room with light. Callidus and Darla both ordered hearty bowls of a rather delicious vegetable beef stew.

Darla swallowed a spoon full of her soup and chuckled, saying, "You gave me such a scare last night!"

"I'm sorry," he replied with a laugh, "but there was little I could do about it."

"You left and all I could think about was you and I and…well, when you got back, I was expecting a little more," she paused, chuckling again, "a bit more pleasant situation."

Half changing the subject, he replied, "What was it, again, that you were thinking about?"

She blushed a bit and became silent for a couple of seconds, picking and poking at a carrot in her soup. "I was thinking…about us."

"Was I too forward last night? I didn't mean to—"

"No, no. You weren't," she interrupted. She smiled again, looking down to avoid his eyes coyly, saying, "It was quite nice, actually."

"Well, I basically told you how I felt last night, in so many words. Now, you tell me," he said, taking a bit more stew.

She was again silent for a few more seconds, the blush returning to her cheeks. "I…" She paused again, but continued, "I have been thinking a lot about you lately. Thinking about Chris, the boy I used to know, and about Callidus, the man who sits before me now. Everything happened so suddenly that I was swept up in my surroundings. Many things bewildered and confused me. When I got down to thinking about us, I realized—"

"That I was still the same annoying, sometimes arrogant, often hated little kid that everyone stayed away from?" he said, sighing a bit.

"No, not at all! I realized that you were still the same sweet, caring, compassionate friend that I had always known, always cared for. I also realized that you were now more than that. I came to see that you were, that you are a leader, our leader, and that you've shown yourself to be a caretaker, a provider, and a guide."

"So, how does this apply to you and me?"

"You've been there for me, for all of us, this past week. In these few short days, so much has happened. It would be easy to lose myself in the moment again, like I almost did last night." She paused again as Callidus' smile dropped. "However, I didn't lose myself in the moment last night. I lost myself in you," she said, reaching across the table to take his hand. She sought his eyes, continuing, "Last night, it hit me, everything. How much it was obvious that you cared for me so deeply, and how much I cared for you. When you kissed me, it was all truth. My doubts dropped away; I didn't need them any longer. I knew in my heart."

He looked into her eyes for a second and smiled softly. "I knew the moment I saw the moonlight cascade off your beautiful face that night on the hammock. I couldn't take my eyes off you." He stood up, both of them basically having finished with their stew, and took her hand. She stood as well and wrapped her arms around his waist, placing her head on his chest.

"I wonder why we never saw this before?" she asked, looking up into his eyes.

"I don't know. We've nearly known each other forever."

"Oh well. Better late than never," she replied, leaning up to kiss him softly.

He kissed her in return and said, "Oh my! I wonder what we're going to tell Donnic and Kailynn."

"Hmm. Well, I've got a feeling Catie, I mean, Kailynn already knows. We gals can tell this kind of thing."

"Yeah, and Donnic's known for a few months now that I've had a crush on you."

"You had a crush on me back home?" she asked, a little bit surprised.

"Yeah, of course. I even got my class schedule switched around last semester so I could be in more classes with you."

She laughed, saying, "No wonder you were in three of my four classes!"

The two of them walked out and down the road back toward the inn, her arm wrapped around his. They reached the fountain in the square and kissed again, in the same spot. They continued to walk, eventually reaching the inn. Donnic and Kailynn were sitting at a table and spotted them coming in.

"Callidus! Glad to see you're back with us. Heard you gave those two quite a beating last night," said Donnic, standing to shake his hand. "How's the arm?"

"It's doing much better, thanks to Darla. What did you find out about those guys?" asked Callidus, sitting at the table. Darla took a seat beside him.

Donnic sat across from them, saying, "Well, I found out that they both had been knocked out. One had a broken jaw and the other had both feet broken. Did you do that? You know I'm the one who's supposed to be doing the butt-kicking in this group."

Callidus chuckled, saying, "Me and my staff took care of the jaw. Davus did the feet, I guess."

"Oh! Well, anyways, I spoke to one of the other castle guards, he was off-duty, but this morning he found out. The night guards supposedly found Davus dead with the two thugs nearby. They aren't sure how Davus managed to get both of them knocked out, but there are rumors along the lines of 'He hit them with a rock' and 'He clubbed them with a stick.' Not much more than that."

"They still have the assassins in custody right?"

"Yeah. They've been questioning them all morning. They're not getting anywhere with them, I don't think. Anyways, Davus will be buried tomorrow." He rolled his eyes and said, scoffing, "Guess who's providing the funeral service?"

Callidus sighed, saying, "Kenather..."

"None other. Though I guess that would really depend on what happens tonight. We're still on, right?"

"Yes, of course. You think I'm going to let something this little slow me down?" asked Callidus with a grin.

"Apparently not," said Donnic. "Well, anyways, I was looking over the message you got this morning again and I had noticed that the words were different," he said, pulling the message from his pocket. He handed it to Callidus.

Callidus read aloud, "'Come to the castle today. Tell them you are the clairvoyant mage I sent for.'" Callidus placed the message inside his robe. "Yes, this is from Cedrick. I will go see him sometime today." He turned to Kailynn. "Everything is ready?"

"Yeah. I finished the last of it this morning. We now have two tents and four bedrolls. I also went to the blacksmith in the castle and got some nails to use as tent pegs. I got some string in the marketplace as well. All we have to do for the tents is string them up between two trees and put them up like a regular tent. We've also got three horses. Penseval's cousin owns a stable and he's arranged to let us take the horses for the next couple of days."

"Good, good. We'll get a bit of food supplies to take with us. We might be able to sneak into Woodsmith and get some stuff as well," said Callidus.

"Looks like all we have left to do is wait. What time are we leaving?" asked Kailynn.

"Well, I want to get set up outside the east gate and wait for his departure. Kailynn, I need you to do a bit of scouting for me. When we're done here, please go out east gate and find some place with adequate cover where we can wait for him."

Kailynn nodded, saying, "Will do, Callidus."

"Donnic, you'll come with me. We're going to see Cedrick together. I don't want to take the chance of another mishap."

"Yes, of course," he replied.

"Darla, you stay here and tend to our stuff. If you think of anything else we're going to need, go ahead and buy it. Be careful, of course," he said, smiling softly to her.

"I will," said Darla, smiling back. Donnic and Kailynn shot a glance at each other, knowingly.

Callidus slipped his hand into his robe and pulled out the watch he brought from home. "It's about three here. Be back here at sundown. I think that'll be about seven o' clock."

The other three nodded and stood. Callidus called his staff to him and he and Donnic walked out. Kailynn stayed behind for a sec to talk to Darla.

"So? Tell me! Tell me!"

"Tell you what?" Darla asked mischievously.

"Well? What happened between you and Callidus today? Don't think I didn't see that look he gave you, not to mention those you gave him. And you never told me what happened last night, either!"

"Nothing, really. We just…talked, that's all," she said.

Kailynn walked over to her, saying, "Sure, sure."

"Well," she paused, "last night, we went for a walk and we just talked a lot." She began to smile widely, suppressing a giddy giggle. "Then he kissed me!"

Kailynn grinned as well, giving her a big hug. "So you two are a thing now?"

"Yeah, I guess we are," she said with a chuckle.

"How did I ever doubt it? You two seem perfect for each other." Donnic and Callidus were on route to the castle, talking as they went. "You know, though, that you can't let this get in the way of your leadership," said Donnic.

"I would never! I care very deeply for Darla, but I care for you and Kailynn in the same amount, just more like a brother and sister."

"I know, I know. But I also know just how one-track your one-track mind can get. When push comes to shove, it's about the team, not about you and Darla."

"I know that, Donnic. I am not about to play favorites, especially when it could mean lives. I may have a one-track mind at times, but

I know when to make the proper decisions."

The two arrived at the castle gate in no time. They presented themselves to the guard, telling him that Callidus was, as expected, the clairvoyant mage here to see McCrary. Donnic, in his warrior garb, easily passed as his personal guard. A guard escorted them inside.

They found themselves first in the grand foyer of the castle. The large, regal room was decorated with tapestries and ornaments, statues and suits of armor, and all sorts of other castle paraphernalia. The guard took them walking down a long, lavish corridor. On each wall were paintings depicting the kings and queens, princes and princesses, and knights of the kingdom's history. Under their feet was a regal red carpet, ornately embroidered in gold.

Eventually, the guard stopped at a door in the hall and knocked abruptly upon it. The door opened and the tired face of Cedrick beckoned them in. The guard motioned for them to enter and then turned to stand watch over the door.

As he shut the door, Cedrick spoke in a fatigued voice, "Hello, young lads. Do not worry about the guard; he is on my side. Please, have a seat."

The two took seats before a large wooden table and glanced around the room. The room had a musty air about it, feeling rather old. The only light provided was through two small windows in the back wall and through a candelabra sitting on the table. There were several bookcases filled to the brims with tomes, some looking new, others looking almost ancient. There was a case against one wall that contained several rather ornate staves. On another wall, there was a beautiful, golden mirror. Cedrick sat on the other side of the table. Callidus asked, "Cedrick, you look very tired. Are you all right?"

"Fear not, Callidus. I am just rather tired. I was up all night trying to squeeze a bit of information from those two brutes in the dungeon. They would not crack."

"I see. Well, I am very sorry about what happened to Davus. I tried to defend him, but—"

"Say no more, lad. I am certain that you did your best to stop them.

My elder colleague, I'm sure, was very proud of the defense you mustered. I was watching through my mirror but would not have been able to get there in time."

"Thank you, Cedrick. How is King Sorrow?"

"He fares no better than yesterday. I would assume that, if the men were sent by Kenather, their defeat helped to distract him for at least the night."

Callidus nodded and said, "I guess we had better get down to business. What were you and Davus going to talk to me about? Oh, and I hope you don't mind Donnic being here. I figured it would have been safer to have him."

The elder nodded, understanding his concern. "We wished to discuss with you the trial you are about to face."

"You mean with Kenather?" asked Donnic, tentatively.

"No, my boy. That is only one piece of the grander scale. What I mean now is the road that you are now on. It certainly is not going to an easy task, lads. I know not precisely what you will face in the days or weeks to come," he said, standing to walk around, "but I know certainly that you will not come out unscathed. The conflict last night is not the last of the conflicts and battles you are to face. It is most certainly not. I do pray that you are prepared, all of you. Your last one, the girl, has she gone through her transformation?"

"Yes. She is now a ranger with a talent for the arrow," said Callidus.

"Good, good. Each of you, your skills, you will each prove invaluable to one another. Never lose the spirit of the team. You were called together, not separately. Keep that in mind always."

The two young men nodded. Cedrick walked around to a bookshelf behind them, taking out an old, dusty tome. He walked back to his table and sat down, splaying the book before him. He continued, "Lads, here I have a very old tome. It was handed down to me by my grandfather. He received it from his grandfather, and so on. We here on the continent of Syerica believe that our world was created eons ago by a being we call 'the Hand.' Centuries ago, there lived a group of wise, wise men. They were given privilege to see what else the Hand had created. He created this world in the beginning and set upon it the spirits of Good and Evil, giving them the power to do with this world what they wished. The Good created the seas, the land, and the life that flourishes upon it.

"However, the Evil would send fires, floods, all kinds of destruction upon the land and the seas to kill the living creatures and plants. The Evil, however, wanted more. More power to destroy, more life to decimate. So he took a step back, so to speak, knowing that the Good would create more. The spirit of Good did, of course. He created man. The Evil began twisting man to his own purposes. The Hand, seeing that his creation was being overrun, turned away from it. He turned away and created a new world, your world."

Callidus and Donnic continued to listen, enthralled at what they were hearing.

Cedrick continued, "He allowed the spirit of Good to influence the new world for ages and ages, only finally allowing the Evil a small foothold. The spirit of Good was much stronger, though, and as able to triumph over the spirit of Evil for eons." He closed the book. "This brings us to today. By and by, the Evil discovered that he could do no more in the other world without more power. So he came back to this world. He returned here to begin draining power from it. My grandfather was the first to discover the resurgence of Evil. He believed it was concentrated, focused somehow, somewhere. He was never able to discover where. In his death, his search ended."

"That explains quite a lot. The little information our tome had told us that the Evil here wishes to gain enough power to enter our world for good," said Callidus.

"Yes, precisely. It is only a matter of time before it has gained enough power. It has to be stopped."

"How, though, are we explained? What made it be the four of us?" asked Donnic.

"I am not precisely sure. It was all forecast in the days of the privileged elders. I would assume that either the Hand or the Good had an influence on this."

"Then we must seek out the Evil and somehow stop its spread, yes?" asked Callidus.

"Yes. How you are to do that? I am not sure. Where you will find it? That I also do not know. I do know that the first rung of the ladder lies in Kenather. If he is under the direction of the Evil, as I am sure he is, then he will no doubt provide us with some manner of clue as to where to seek the Evil. Be that through his capture or through his death, only you can tell."

"Then we shall see what becomes of the Archpriest," said Donnic, patting the hilt of his sword.

"Yes, yes. Certainly. Do, however, be very careful. As it is, I do not quite know the reaches of Kenather's power. I know he must certainly be very powerful, however, and I am not sure that you can match up to him. I do pray you can."

The two nodded. Cedrick stood, motioning for them to do the same. He walked around and shook both of their hands. He paused at Callidus, saying, "You, my lad, are going to be very crucial to your friends. You must lead them well. I believe you will be a great sorcerer, it is your destiny."

"Thank you, Cedrick. I shall never forget your words."

The two were shown to the door and back down the lavish hallway.

The group reassembled in the inn about an hour before expected, so they took some time to rest up, just lounging around in the tavern. Kailynn had found a bit of a gully, a few hundred yards outside of the east gate. The gate was situated a bit closer to the castle, higher up on the hill. The gully would be technically visible from the gate, but it had some rock cover which would provide them with a good place to watch the gate without being seen. The guys shared with the girls their conversation with Cedrick, giving them the gist of the story.

As the sun began to set, they started sorting their equipment, placing the rolled bedrolls, folded tents, and blankets inside the large bag and tying it off. They gathered themselves up and bid a farewell to Pense, walking out into the street. They headed to the marketplace and were able to round up some vegetables, bread, and a bit of boar meat. They got a pot and a pan from a merchant as well. Darla cast her preservation ward over the supplies and wrapped them in some spare cloth, setting them inside the big bag.

"Let's go out the south gate. I don't doubt that Kenather's got connections all over town," said Donnic. "The stables are on our way there."

"Good idea," said Callidus, as they headed south from the inn. "We can still get to the gully if we go this way, right, Kailynn?"

"Oh, of course. There shouldn't be any problem."

The group headed to the south gate, getting their horses and passing by the guards without problem. They turned off the main path and followed Kailynn toward the gully. By the time the sun had reached the horizon, they had reached their hideout. Callidus tied their horses to a tree near the gully and the four sat down behind the rocks and began to wait, taking turns watching for the archpriest's departure. Travelers came and went, but none strayed off the path leading away from the east gate. Within the hour, the sun had set and the field beyond the castle was darkened, the two moons providing their only light.

"What do you think will happen tonight, Callidus?" asked Darla. Callidus and Kailynn sat with her while Donnic kept the first watch.

"Well, I think it's going to be a very dangerous period of time. We're going to have to be quite cautious as we follow Kenather. We have to stay close enough to see him but far enough behind to not be seen by him."

"You know, I could trail him myself while you guys follow at a safe distance," said Kailynn. "I'm certain I can move without being seen. I was able to get out the gate without the guards even hearing my footsteps this afternoon."

"That would be a good idea," said Donnic, turning around and motioning to Darla to continue watch. They switched places as Darla took a seat just behind the rocks to watch the gate. "It wouldn't be good to get into a confrontation with Kenather before we have the chance to find out anything."

"Good point, Donnic. Kailynn, once we see him leave, you wait a while then start following him. We'll wait about five or ten minutes the follow as well. If he strays from the road any, you leave some rocks as a marker and we'll follow accordingly. Otherwise, find us outside of the village. I'm certain you can."

Kailynn nodded, saying, "You can count on me." She stood up and walked over to the horses, taking a brush that Penseval's cousin gave them and brushing the horses down. They were grazing lightly on the grass nearby.

"How would you suggest we go about fighting this guy, Donnic? I'm assuming he's going to have some power up his sleeves," said Callidus.

"Well, we could go for the old 'find a weakness' ploy, but I doubt we'll have time. Once he's onto us, it's going to be hectic. What can you do to him with the spells you have?"

Callidus reached into the air and pulled out the spell tome, flipping through to the spells he had transcribed. "I've got the element manipulations and a blindness spell. I've also got a repair orb in my pouch, just in case something gets broken."

"If he's any kind of mage, I doubt he'll be susceptible to very much. He's probably very strong against mind and body magic, so the blindness spell might not do too much good. What are the manipulations going to be good for?"

"Hmm. The earth spell can create rocks and whatnot. I can magically chuck a rock at his head. I might be able to throw him off his guard with a minor tremble, but not much more with that one." He flipped the page, looking over the next spell. "Well, with this water manipulation, I can get him wet and hope he catches pneumonia, but that's a bit unlikely," he said with a chuckle.

"Is there anything it can do?" asked Donnic, unsheathing his sword and polishing it a bit with the cloth of his tunic.

"Well, I might be able to use it and the earth spell together to create a mud bog, but not a very big one. I might be able to freeze the water, too, if I combine it with the air spell." He closed the tome and placed it at his side.

Donnic nodded, replacing his sword in its sheath. "Well, if you see an opportunity, take it. I'll try and cue you if I think of anything. I hope he's not protected against any elements; otherwise we're really screwed. We're just really going to have to be careful to avoid his magic, if any of it is avoidable."

The other two nodded. Kailynn walked back over and sat with the group. After an hour had passed, Darla placed Kailynn on watch and walked over to where Callidus was seated, snuggling up beside him to get a bit more warmth. He wrapped his arm around her, noticing that the chill of the night air was beginning to set in while they waited for any sign of their target.

Callidus and Donnic had continued to talk about the night and what they might face from Kenather. "If anything, I can at least distract Kenather while you and Kailynn go at him," said Callidus.

"What do you want me to do, Donnic?" asked Darla.

"Well, let's see. What spells do you have?" he asked.

Callidus handed her the tome from his side and she opened it to look through her spells. "I don't seem to have very much that will be of use to us. I've got my wards for our traveling, but they're not going to do any good in battle. I've got the confusion spell and the light element. Could those be used?"

"Hmm. Like I told Callidus, I'm not sure how much good some of the minor body and mind spells like confusion and blindness will do, but they are at least a couple more spells to pull out."

"The light spell, any way we can use that, Don?" asked Callidus.

"Maybe. The whole creating balls of light might work, but I really can't think of how those affect the body. Maybe it's just one of those magic things. Any combos you can pull, Callidus?"

"Maybe. The air spell makes some sparks and static electricity. We could use those as a distraction by adding some colored light or something like that. I really can't think of much else."

"Well, distractions are good," said Donnic. "I just wish we knew more about the guy. I mean, you're run-of-the-mill thief or murderer is easy to take care of. Couple of good slashes, they're dispatched. Magic makes it a whole new ball game. It's like taking a normal—"

"He's out," interrupted Kailynn, watching the gate carefully.

They turned toward her as she spoke. "He's traveling by horse. He's stopped at the gate and is talking to the guards."

About five minutes later, he took off at a trot down the path leading away. Kailynn waited just long enough to put some scouting distance between them then set out on foot, insisting that a horse would make her easier to spot and that she could handle keeping up without a problem. Callidus gave them about seven or eight minutes, both persons no longer being visible, and gathered the group, mounting the horses and setting out.

In no time, the group saw a little bit of light in the distance. They were riding through a bit of wooded countryside. As they got closer, it became apparent that they were looking at Woodsmith Village. They pulled off the main road into the trees nearby and dismounted. The group waited for Kailynn.

"Here you guys are," said a voice stepping out from the trees, spooking Darla and making her jump. It was Kailynn, coming nearly undetected through the shadows.

"Wow, you're really good at that," said Darla.

"What did you find out, Kailynn?" asked Callidus.

Kailynn walked over to the rest of the group, saying, "He is staying at a small house on the far end of town, opposite this end. I didn't see anyone else in the house or with him, though. As he entered the town, there were a few people that seemed to recognize him, but they kind of avoided him."

"All right," Callidus said, "it's going to be all up to what he does from here. Kailynn, what was he doing before you left?"

"He was going to sleep," she replied.

"Good. I hate to ask this, but I need you to go check on him every couple of hours. You're probably the only one who knows quite how to prowl well enough."

She nodded, saying, "Of course. Not a problem."

The group set up camp, pitching their tents, tying up the horses, etc. Callidus and Donnic gathered wood for a fire and Callidus sparked it up using an air spell. Darla planted her staff near the fire and cast the creature ward upon it as a beacon. They sat around the fire, talking about their adventure so far and about what they would do in the time to come. The air was getting colder as the night progressed, and each person wrapped tighter in his or her cloak, except Darla, who was more concerned about wrapping herself in Callidus' arms.

It was getting well into the night and they decided to sleep until morning, each person taking a watch. Callidus started out on watch, letting Kailynn and the others sleep and keeping the fire built up. After a couple of hours had passed, Callidus walked over to the girls tent and woke both Darla and Kailynn up, sending Kailynn to check on Kenather and putting Darla on watch.

As Kailynn headed out, Callidus stayed out just a bit to talk to Darla by the fire. They conversed about various things before a large yawn from Callidus prompted her to send him off to bed. In course of time, Kailynn returned and went back to bed. After another watch had passed, Darla woke Donnic and bade him take his turn at watch.

The morning came with Callidus on his second watch. Donnic took a bit of extra time with his, not needing very much rest to refresh spell casting abilities as the two mages and not having to get up every couple of hours like Kailynn. Callidus sat, tending the now dying fire, not bothering to keep it up much longer as the sun was about to crest. Donnic woke up again, coming out of their tent and heading over to Callidus, taking a seat beside him on the ground.

"What's on the agenda for today, Calli?" asked Donnic.

"You shouldn't be up yet. You've barely gotten any sleep tonight."

"I don't really need much sleep. You know that."

"Understandable. I'm not much of a heavy sleeper, either," Callidus said, prodding one of the logs with a stick.

"Anyway, what are we going to try and do today?"

"Well, for the most part, we need to do some reconnaissance on Kenather. We can try and ask around in the village for some information. We just don't need to do so as a group. We don't want to get anyone suspicious. If Kenather knows about us, he knows about all of us, so he'll be expecting all of us."

"Yeah, that makes sense. Well, want to fix some breakfast for the girls?"

"Sure. You slice up a bit of the boar and I'll toast some of the bread."

"All right," Donnic replied, heading over to the horses. He took the large bag, untying it from the saddle and brought it over to the fire.

Callidus had gone to grab a few more pieces of wood to refresh the fire. After he had it flaming up again, he sat thinking how he was going to put the food over the fire. *I could try to hang it off of something*, he thought. *Nothing to hang it from, though. Hmm...* He sat, looking at the fire.

"If only we had a stovetop," said Donnic, picking up on Callidus' dilemma.

Callidus brightened up, saying, "That's it!" He raised his hand over the fire and started chanting. The dirt surrounding the fire began to shift a little bit, rising up and solidifying into a bit of a rock stand over the fire. He swept the stand clean of dirt, reached into the large bag, and took out a half-loaf of bread, placing it atop the stand. It held sturdy. Callidus removed the bread and took the dagger from his robe, cutting off a few slices and laying them on the stone. He felt it begin to get hot.

"Ingenious use of magic, Mr. Lanstone," said Donnic.

"Thank you, Mr. Turnblade," said Callidus.

Donnic began slicing up a bit of the boar meat, forming some bacon-esque strips. He looked over, noticing Callidus turning over the bread with his fingers and dagger. The side now on top had begun to brown. Donnic rewrapped the meat and brought the strips over to the stand, taking the pan from the nearby bag and placing it on the other side of the stand. He placed some of the strips on it, watching them start to sizzle. Callidus took out some of the spare cloth and sat it on the ground, placing the toasted bread on it. The boar bacon was also finished in no time, sending out a strong, rugged aroma into the air.

It wasn't a few seconds after everything was finished that the girls awakened, coming out of their tent with yawns. "Oh, you fixed breakfast for us. That's so sweet," said Kailynn, standing and walking over to the fire, sitting back down. Darla followed shortly, sitting next to Callidus.

"Hope you like bacon and toast," said Donnie, borrowing Callidus' dagger to spear a couple of pieces to put on each slice of toast. Callidus handed a slice to both the girls then took one himself as Donnic sat beside him, taking a slice also.

"Wow, I like what you did with the makeshift stove there, guys," said Darla, breaking the toast in half and making a sandwich. She took a bite and smiled.

"It was Callidus' handicraft, I just cooked," said Donnic, doing the same with his bread.

"Yes. Hopefully the spells will refresh by nightfall. I still have at least two more goes with them anyways," he said.

After breakfast, the group took turns going into the village to find out whatever they could about Kenather. It basically seemed as if the whole village was aware of his presence but didn't really know about what he was doing there or anything else, for that matter. When Donnic asked a few people about the Forest of Night, he got very strange reactions. Most people refused to talk about it. A few had their own little spook stories to tell about one family member seeing this or a next door neighbor's cousin's best friend's dog getting lost. Nothing important was turned up, however. The only pertinent thing they learned was that the forest was no more than a ten-minute walk outside of town.

The remainder of the day passed very slowly. With nothing to do, the group mostly sat around and talked. Callidus and Darla took a walk in the nearby forest, doing a bit of kissing, but nothing more. Callidus and Donnic started up a staff fight, using his and Darla's staves, to give them both some practice with the weapon. It lasted for a little bit before a nice move from Donnic knocked the wind out of Callidus. The two girls went off and talked for a bit, mostly about the two guys. The group even took a small side trip to see the Forest of

Night before nightfall. Just as they were told, the forest was barren and sparse. It was as if the autumn had swept over the trees and stole away each leaf from every branch. Had they spent enough time peering through, they probably would have seen the other end of the forest through the lifeless wood.

All in all, the whole group was glad to see the sunset. Kailynn went to spy on Kenather and wait for him to make a move. Around midnight, Kenather departed from the house and headed east, towards the Forest of Night. Kailynn returned and the group gathered most of their things. Kailynn readied her bow and quiver and strapped them to her back. Donnic donned his armor and sheathed his sword. They left the horses tied up at the campsite, as well as the large bag full of items, which they hung from a tree. Darla refreshed her preservation and repellent wards just in case. They headed out toward the forest, Kailynn several feet ahead in the shadows, scouting out their path. It wasn't long until they reached the edge.

Before them now rose a massive forest, almost a jungle, with vines streaking out all over the place, a large amount of underbrush, split only by the small path leading inward. The trees rose high above their eyes, forming a dense canopy of tropical green which was unbefitting to the rather temperate trees that were found elsewhere in the area. The lifeless grove which they had visited earlier had exploded in green. Darla waved her hand near the ground and a small sheen of light straddled their path, leading them as they walked inward. The ominous forest was black and haunting, filled with the sounds of buzzing insects and calling animals. The noise wasn't so much overpowering as it was entangling, giving them a nervous sense of being surrounded by unknown things.

Donnic unsheathed his sword and stepped in front of the group, hacking at various vines and things that had spread their way across the path. The forest seemed to be alive, to be moving, breathing, pulsing around them. As they traveled onward, the path got more rugged. Kailynn stepped off the path on accident and got her leg caught in a vine. As she reached down to untangle it, she realized that it was wrapping itself tighter around her! She quickly whipped a dagger from her belt, chopping the vine just past her leg. It flailed for a second before withering and dying around her leg. She pulled it off and rushed back into the center of the group. They continued along the path, staying close together. Callidus handed Kailynn his long dagger, knowing that she wouldn't be able to draw an arrow soon enough to handle anything. The four kept walking, eventually noticing that the path became wider and wider.

Though the four tried to keep their noise down to a minimum, the rustle of their feet in the undergrowth was still audible along with the rest of the noise in the wood. Kailynn's ears soon perked up, however, as she detected another noise, just faintly behind the group. She stopped, nearly causing Darla to bump into her.

"What is it, Kailynn?" she asked.

"There's something following us; it's just beyond the darkness."

The four turned and peered into the shadows, seeing little but the fearsome foliage they had already passed through. All of a sudden, a howl pierced the night! Two glowing yellow eyes began to approach, growing brighter as they stalked towards the group. Donnic drew his sword and Kailynn, the dagger, Callidus and Darla sporting their staves. The eyes were soon accompanied by the glimmer of dripping, hungry teeth against Darla's light. The approaching figure suddenly lunged forward, toppling Darla and Callidus. Strangely, though Callidus' staff was knocked from his hand, Darla's hands seemed to stay glued in hers so instinctively she swung at the beast. As she began to make contact, she noticed a bit of rope with a small piece of leather tied round its neck.

Donnic and Kailynn caught their first glimpse of the beast, a wolf-like canine, though larger than its counterpart, covered in bushy black fur, snarling as it was knocked aside. Donnic quickly dove toward the animal, catching its hind leg with his blade. The beast yelped and swung back around, attempting to latch onto Donnic's bracer. As it tore a bit of the leather with its rather sharp teeth, it was quickly struck by Callidus' staff firmly against the neck. A savage crack escaped from the bones causing the creature to drop. As its body heaved with a faint few breaths, it began to shrink into what appeared to be a common Doberman. As Donnic and Darla checked their clothes and armor for damage, Callidus and Kailynn stooped to examine the animal. The rope and leather turned out to be a bit of a collar and tag, the words "Jumper, Woodsmith Vill." etched into the leather.

"Apparently not all of the villagers' stories were that untrue," said Callidus lowly.

Darla and Donnic appeared to have little more than a few scratches and tears. Neither was bleeding, so Darla chose to save her healing spell for another time. The four gathered themselves together, deciding to leave the dog where it was, and continued on down the path.

Suddenly they stopped. In the distance, a faint light was glowing.

"Kailynn, go check that out. Be careful," said Callidus.

She replied with a nod and dropped to the ground, launching herself forward with silent, cat-like ease. She darted ahead of them until she was no longer visible.

So that's how she does that, thought the other three almost simultaneously.

Shortly she returned to the group, telling them that there was a clearing ahead of them. Kenather was standing in the center of it, waving his hands around, chanting. "He was apparently trying to open a portal of some nature," she said.

"All right. Let's move forward. Darla, dissolve the light spell," replied Callidus. She did as instructed, but immediately took hold of Callidus' hand. Their night vision came to them after a short time and they headed toward the light they saw ahead, very slowly and as quietly as possible.

As they approached the clearing, it became clear that Kenather had succeeded in opening the portal and was now talking into it. The portal was little more than a swirl of clouds and a glimmer of what appeared to be glass, casting a translucent reflection of the archpriest and his surroundings. The priest stood tall and thin, wrapped in his white priest's robes, wearing the hood to cover his head and face. In between what Kenather said, there would come a minor rumble from within the portal, to which Kenather would respond again. As they got closer, they began to be able to hear what Kenather was saying.

"No, my liege. Only two weeks left. I'm certain he will be dead by then."

"He must be talking about the king," Donnic whispered. The four of them stopped and crouched in a position that didn't really give either the portal or the priest a line of sight, unless they were being directly looked upon.

After a rumble, he continued. "Yes, I made sure to forge the new corpora. The throne now defaults to the advisor in the king's absence. Once I'm there, I will give the people to you."

"He's planning to take over!" whispered Callidus.

Another rumble followed and they heard him laugh, saying, "You're mistaken, my lord. The old man can't get in my way. I already took care of the one. The other will follow if he doesn't bend to our will. He knows that well." A rumble brought down his spirit and he replied, "No, no, we didn't catch the guy. So he took out two assassins, he was probably just a passerby, and people willing to sell their morals for a few gold coins are in no short supply. If I need another, I'll get another."

"Damn him, he did hire those assassins, we were right," said Callidus. Darla squeezed his hand.

"All the preparations are complete. I've already had the court blacksmith create a new insignia ring for my reign. He knows what will happen to him if he tells anyone, so I'm safe." A rumble interrupted him but he quickly replied, "No, I didn't leave it at the castle, Master. I'm not that stupid. It's there in my bag," he said, motioning to a small sack just a few feet away.

"That's it!" whispered Darla. "That's the proof we need, right Callidus?"

"Yes, somehow we have to get that ring from him," he replied.

"How are we going to do that?" Kailynn asked. "I'm not certain

I can get to him without being seen and I can't properly fire an arrow unless I stand."

"We might just have to fight him for it," said Donnic. "Callidus, we need to make some kind of diversion."

"You're right," he replied. He thought for a second then turned to Darla. "How far away can you make a ball of light?"

"No, I already used the—oh wait, it just came back to me. How odd. I can make it a few yards, I'm sure. Why?"

"Okay, if you make a ball of light as far away as possible, I'll create a wind gust to toss it across the forest. That will distract Kenather. How do we get to him then, Donnic?"

"Well, with that distraction, Kailynn can try and nail him with an arrow."

"What happens if that doesn't work?" asked Darla

"Well, then just throw whatever you've got at him and we'll go from there."

"All right. Here goes nothing," said Darla. She raised her hand toward the forest beyond Kenather and focused her energy on creating distance. Callidus raised his hands as well, getting ready to push the ball away. As soon as the first instance of light began to show, Callidus flung his hands forward and the now baseball-sized light was blown away, bouncing off trees before coming to land.

Kenather quickly noticed the light and closed the portal, turning to go investigate. Kailynn jumped to her feet, took out her bow, armed an arrow, and let fly. The archpriest turned around to see the arrow flying toward him and stood still, closing his eyes. The arrow hit his robe just at his lower ribs, but it bounced off! He quickly raised his hands and began to chant, a wave of almost electrical purple light washing over Kailynn. She froze in place, not being able to move or speak.

Donnic rushed at him, sword in hand, only to be knocked over by a blast of energy from Kenather's palm. Darla waved her hands to cast confusion over his mind, but the spell was turned away, reflected back onto Darla. She dropped to her knees, his mind muddled and clouded.

"You fools! Who are you to come at me?" the archpriest shouted, a terrible laugh escaping his lips.

Callidus quickly threw up his hands, a minor torrent of water rushing from them, spraying all over the tall man. He simply laughed and reached inside his robe, pulling out a spell orb.

"Your little tricks amuse me, Wizard. It is time, however, for the four of you to say goodbye!" He raised the orb above his head and began chanting. The orb soon glowed and sizzled with power, sparks flying around it as a ball of electricity slowly concentrated itself in his hands. He didn't realize however that his first spell had worn off and an arrow was shot straight into the orb from Kailynn's bow. The orb shattered in a blinding flash, energy flying out, down into Kenather's body forcing a massive scream of pain from his mouth. As the electricity surged through his bones, his face contorted in a ghastly and hideous visage of pain and his screams tore into the night, horrifying shrieks of torture. He quickly dropped to the ground, his body charred and mangled, no life left in his veins. Donnic had gotten back up to his feet and Callidus walked over to Darla, helping her up. The spell was beginning to wear off as her senses came back to her. The four met around Kenather's lifeless body. The robes he bore were no more than ashes still smoldering. The smell of his burnt flesh was nauseating to the four. Callidus picked up Kenather's bag, finding within a few smaller pouches of gold, a key, presumably to the house he was staying in, a few scrolls, a few orbs, and the small, gold insignia ring.

Walking away from the clearing, the group stayed close together, and mostly silent. Callidus contemplated what happened when the orb was broken, and wondered if that could happen to him or Darla as well. The horrific thought of the man being destroyed by his own magic was enough to make Callidus nauseous as he stooped to compose himself. Darla stood beside him, understanding his thoughts and wrapped her arms around him, providing him some substance of comfort. Callidus now understood the risk he ran by wielding such power.

He motioned to the others that he was all right and stood up, grasping Darla's hand as they began to walk again. In no time they reached their campsite and packed up, not caring about the hour, just wishing to get back to the castle walls.

In the middle of the night, they had reached the city and found Cedrick in the castle. They explained everything and gave the insignia ring to him. Looking through the scrolls, they also found the spell that the archpriest had used on the king and quickly sought an antidote from the vaults of the library, even though the librarian wasn't happy to have been gotten up. In no time, the king was restored to health and was told the entire story. By the time the sun had broken the horizon, the king had called the entire town to the castle and announced, from the balcony, what happened. The people were set buzzing with the news and applauded when the four were brought out onto the balcony.

Davus was given a proper funeral, officiated by the king. Callidus spoke a few words, as did Cedrick. He was then interned in the castle tomb.

At the grand reception following, nearly the whole castle court, as well as every important person in town was present. Penseval was invited as well as the castle blacksmith and both were given seats near the four. The town guard had lined up behind along the wall behind the king, the head of the guard placed directly behind the royal head. The king, once more, told of the heroics of the four. With Cedrick at his side, he announced several important things.

"The royal advisor and I wish, again, to thank you, Callidus, Donnic, Darla, and Kailynn for saving my life and my kingdom. The late Advisor Berron would also be greatly proud. Have you decided what you will do next, young lad?" he asked, turning to Callidus.

"Well, actually, we don't know. Until we can get some kind of clue as to where to go next, we really don't have anything to seek out."

"Then you shall remain in the castle with me. Callidus and Darla, for your astounding effort in your spell casting, you shall be given an apprenticeship to Cedrick. He will train you well."

Cedrick smiled and nodded, walking over to stand behind Callidus and Darla.

King Sorrow turned to Donnic, saying, "For your heroism in rushing headlong against the evil archpriest, I've arranged to have Jamiken Partreon, an old companion of mine who fought beside me in the Gammeron War decades ago, to come and train you with the sword. He's one of the greatest swordsmen in my kingdom." Donnic smiled, bowing his head to the king.

He turned finally to Kailynn, saying, "And you, brave archer. I'm granting you the position of deputy captain of the castle guard for as long as you remain here." The guard captain who talked to Kailynn earlier nodded his consent. "I'm also going to see to getting you some enchantments to use with your arrows."

The grand feast continued on into the night with celebrations and parties held in the heroes' honor.

Printed in the United States
16756LVS00001B/157-204